BOUND

by Hannah Pike

First published by
Scott Martin Productions, 2019
www.scottmartinproductions.com

First published in Great Britain in 2019 by
Scott Martin Productions
10 Chester Place,
Adlington, Chorley, PR6 9RP
scottmartinproductions@gmail.com
www.scottmartinproductions.com

Electronic version available for purchase on Amazon.
Copyright (c) Hannah Pike and Scot Martin Productions.

Cover art from pngtree.

Acknowledgements

With special thanks to:
Anna Tripp
Penny Pritchard

Darren Elliott-Smith
Hanah Ahmet
Emily Cooper

Marymay Conway
Helen Manning
Lesley Atherton

Dedication

To my amazing and supportive parents,
Andrew Pike & Louise Pike

The Castle: Waking Up

Emma could only run as fast as her legs would carry her, which wasn't long - not while she was in this state and while her arm and legs were aching from the bruises he left earlier that night.

She was running away from him, the one who had turned her into a person she despised with every fibre of her being - this submissive girl who had been introduced to her unwanted slave-like existence.

Ignoring the rain lashing down from the sky, she was grateful for the water seeping through her clothes, cooling and energising her.

Emma was grateful for that, but she was so tired. If only she could rest her eyes just for a minute...

With one careless fall, her body suddenly tumbled onto the pavement like a discarded, lifeless doll.

They were getting closer - she could feel it.

She scrambled to her feet and saw the blood oozing from her cuts to mix with the rain on the cobblestones beneath her.

Staring at the strange pink mixture on the ground, black spots appeared in her vision.

No, not now...

With a whimper of defiance from her lips, she heard the footsteps approaching.

Then there was nothing.

Emma

Emma woke up with a jolt, her heart racing.

She was having the weird dreams again – likely a by-product of her insomnia. Yes, more than likely, as her snowy white sheets were messed up and out of place.

All the stuffed animals that she normally slept with were strewn on the other side of the room, along with the second pillow she'd cling to each night for comfort.

She'd been lashing out again.

Well, at least it meant she got some decent sleep. Insanely, she never did unless she was stuck in a nightmare.

Sighing to herself at the messy results of the previous night's dreaming, she got up and picked up all her stuffed animals along with her pillow and put them all back in their rightful positions on the newly-made bed.

It wasn't like she was getting back to sleep now.

Rubbing her eyes, she opened her mauve curtains and opened her window to let some fresh air in. Hopefully it would help her sleep better that night. Anything was worth a try, and she was pretty sure that she'd read it somewhere in a self-help for insomnia article.

The trance of her thoughts was broken by a flashing light coming from somewhere in her room. It reflected onto the ceiling and blinked every few seconds.

She was an idiot for getting freaked out! It was probably just her phone that she'd left lying around.

Following the blinking, she found the phone

on the floor by her tall, cream bookshelves and partly hidden under the drawers that contained all the art supplies she hadn't touched in a few months.

Realising that the phone was probably on critical battery, she picked it up and plugged it into by her bed but decided to ignore whatever messages she had. She'd deal with them later.

Beginning to get fidgety and shaky, Emma knew that her next step must be to take her pills.

She opened a desk drawer gently. A little of the white paint had begun to flake off and the whole drawer seemed, as it if could collapse at any moment.

Her hands eventually grasped her sought-for item and she pulled it out of the drawer.

Shaking the plastic jar, the contents of which cast off an eerie green glow, she allowed herself to sigh heavily.

Emma would have to get more soon.

In her hands was the prescription that helped her deal with her insomnia, at times when it was critically bad. She had already tried the cognitive behaviour therapy program, but that didn't stop the endless nights of sweating, shaking and screaming.

She would need to refill the prescription soon.

Running a hand through her long blonde hair, she was shocked at its clumpy, greasy feel. It was as if it hadn't been in washed in days. She grimaced.

How could she forget to take care of herself?

The dark circles under her eyes registered their dull protest as she looked at herself in her full-length mirror.

What would her friends think if they saw her now?

The fashion-obsessed Emma now looked as if she'd just crawled out of an alleyway, broken and defeated.

But Emma didn't want to think about them right now. She would fix herself up with make-up, a shower and most importantly, caffeine.

Her phone vibrated in protest at her ignorance. She glared at it from the other side of the room, then sighed and picked it up.

But she wouldn't check it yet. She would take it downstairs with her and check a little later.

Today was her first day back at college, and she needed to get everything sorted out for herself before she even thought about other people.

Her phone lit up again and displayed the time.

It was six in the morning. No wonder it was so bleak and quiet outside.

Emma knew that her dad had left to go on a business trip for a couple of weeks, which meant she had the house all to herself for a good while.

She winced at the crustiness of her lips and decided to head downstairs with the kitchen in mind. She was dying for a cup of tea or any form of caffeine that could help wake her up.

Going through the normal processes of filling up the kettle and putting it on to boil, she opened the pine cupboards and retrieved her favourite Scorpio mug from inside.

The mug had been her favourite for years - since back when she was a proud astrology nerd. Her parents had bought it for her while she was on holiday, back when things were happier.

Maybe that's why she loved it so much.

Clenching the handle of the mug, she filled it with boiling water.

She slipped a little milk in and gave the tea a quick stir before removing the teabag.

She was going to miss having days on end to try and catch up with missing sleep.

Taking a long gulp of her tea, she sighed in contentment as it ran down her throat and warmth suffused every part of her body.

That was when she finally took the time to check her phone and discovered that she had been added into a chat with her old friends and two guys that she didn't know.

Probably two guys that her old friends had picked up at a club or something.

They were inviting her to Mia's birthday party that night. It was to be a club outing, of course.

Her friends hadn't changed much.

Okay, sure, count me in.

Emma typed the reply quickly and sent it just as fast - before she had a chance to change her mind.

She needed this.

This was an opportunity to appear normal - and she'd take it.

Heading upstairs, she flicked through all the clothing in her wardrobe, trying to find something to wear, both for the day at college, and the night out. But the contents of her wardrobe were dry and bland.

Nothing in there filled her with confidence.

Pushing that thought aside, she finished her tea in two gulps and forced herself to pick out an outfit for college at least.

What she had lying crease-free on her ironing board would have to do. The outfit consisted of a black band shirt and jeans of the same shade.

She went through her daily cleaning routine and made sure her hair was decent. Two more items crossed off her list.

Slipping her shoes on, she grabbed her bag and left the house.

Walking up to the college brought back so

many memories, especially when she headed inside.

They sent her a new temporary college pass to use until they knew that she was going to stay longer than a few weeks. It was fair enough after everything that had happened in her life.

Dealing with the destruction of her family hadn't been easy and she'd had to pull her dad and herself back to some sense of normality. Besides, she had no other choice at the time: she couldn't let herself and her family fade away into nothing.

Pulling her phone from her coat pocket, she sent a text to her group of college friends checking if they were all meeting up at their usual spot.

Her phone vibrated a few minutes later with a message in return:

Yeah. Same spot.

Even after a year, Emma still remembered everything from the first and only college year that she had. Before it all went to hell.

Heading inside and ignoring a few stares from former tutors, she made her way up the stairs and over to the booth she knew way too well.

Seeing the group together again filled her with an unanticipated sense of dread.

She would make an effort this time.

'You're late,' Mia announced in a condescending tone, staring at her with sapphire blue eyes that always pulled guys in. That and her wavy, natural blonde hair of course.

Emma wasn't surprised at how many guys swooned and fell at Mia's feet.

Quite literally, sometimes.

Today, Mia had opted to wear an aqua blue and white striped crop top paired with denim shorts and canvas shoes.

'I know,' Emma sighed. 'I woke up late. You

know that I have problems sleeping.'

They didn't know that to the full extent.

'Chill out Ash, Emma hasn't been around for a year. Give her a break, OK?' Zoey piped up in support.

So, they were going to address the elephant in the room?

Zoey was pretty much wearing the same thing as Mia but instead of an aqua blue and white crop top, it was a bright sunshine yellow and cream.

The only difference between them really was Zoey's ginger hair which swung back and forth in a ponytail every time she moved.

'Oh yeah, that's right, she hasn't been around for a year.'

Mia glared at Emma.

So, they were going to address it.

What exactly could Emma say?

'I-' Emma started, and was then cut off by Mia.

'Whatever... Anyway, I have news.'

That was it? They weren't going to probe her some more or ask her anything else?

She was partly relieved, and partly disappointed.

But at least it was over for now.

'Ben finally asked me out!'

Mia was grinning from ear to ear, blissfully happy and ignoring the complete silence from the others.

'Ben? Like Ben in our year?'

Emma raised an eyebrow, questioning this whole situation. She could have sworn that Zoey had a thing for that Ben. If it was him that Mia was talking about, Zoey needed to step up and make a move.

Zoey always been the meek one between two feisty girls. Perhaps their feistiness was why Emma and Mia had always clashed so much.

Mia simply laughed as if Emma had said something impossible.

'No! God!'

She pulled a face of disgust.

'He's *older.*'

Mia was talking as if the identity of her new man was blatantly obvious. She also had a weird loved-up look in her eyes.

Maybe it was more lust than anything, but Emma couldn't place it at all.

'Oh,' was all Emma could say in this situation, but she did manage to nod supportively.

It was then that Zoey joined the conversation.

'His friend is pretty hot too.'

'And single,' Mia commented, winking at her.

So *that's* what tonight was about.

Was Emma just intruding on hook-up plans or was tonight perhaps about showing her what she had missed – or even setting her up?

'Hey, guys, I'll see you later, I have lessons,' she murmured, throwing them apologetic looks. The others just nodded to her and told her that they'd see her later and went back to being absorbed in their own conversations. Just as Emma was absorbed with her own thoughts.

They didn't care if she left. She knew that.

Getting all her things together, Emma headed into the classroom.

Trying to ignore all the stares she was getting from her classmates, she sat in the seat that she always used to sit in at the back-left corner of the room.

She had decided all those years ago that it was

easier to be secluded so that she could just get on with her work without any interruptions.

It didn't take her much to get through the first task that they had been set. She plunged into her work with enthusiasm.

The college day had left Emma feeling satisfied. Her tutors had been helpful and given her decent feedback on her assignments. Deciding to walk home, she noticed the darkness beginning to set in and began to panic.

Remembering the skills her therapist had taught her, she stopped moving and took a few minutes to focus on breathing in through her nose and out through her mouth.

She unzipped her coat pocket and pulled out her set of keys, holding the sharpest few between her fingers while pushing a button on her phone and watching as her torch came alive to shed a bit of light on the surrounding area.

She could do this.

It was all in her mind.

Just her mind.

Relief washed over her as she reached the pathway that she knew would lead her right to her house.

She was okay, and she was safe.

Emma repeated that like a mantra in her head as she unlocked her door and went inside. She slammed the door shut behind herself.

Once she was satisfied that everything was secure, she pulled out a ready meal from the freezer and stuck it in the microwave to cook. It wasn't her favourite, but it would do.

By the time it had finished cooking she'd have

decided what she was going to wear tonight.

Her phone vibrated with texts from the group chat.

What time do you want us to pick you up? This was from Zoey.

You're not bailing on us, right? read another from Mia.

Emma fired two texts back. The first was to Zoey letting her know that seven would be a good time to be picked up. The second was to Mia assuring her that she was still coming.

The pinging noise coming from the kitchen indicated that her dinner was cooked.

Selecting an outfit would have to wait until later.

Emma went into the kitchen, grabbed a fork from her drawer and sorted everything out to eat.

A few hours later, she had eaten and was ready to go out and have a good time.

In the end she'd selected to wear a vermillion red tassel dress matched with nude tights and scarlet red heels.

She slipped on her leather jacket and put her bag on her shoulder. She was finally ready to be collected.

Emma: Friendships

When Mia and Zoey arrived at her front door, they were clearly already completely drunk out of their minds. My God, it looked as if they couldn't even walk properly by the way they were swaying gently from side to side. They did this even while supposedly standing still.

They even had to lean against each other and the side of the wall and buildings in order to stay upright.

But at least they hadn't fallen to the floor as yet. Perhaps she had that to look forward to later in the night.

Zoey was wearing a cobalt blue top that stopped just above the bottom of her chest and she'd paired this with denim shorts, finishing off the outfit with high heels. It didn't look great as an outfit, but the shorts did look good on her.

But then again, Emma didn't really think she would care about that, given how drunk she was.

Mia had opted to wear something different to Zoey tonight, and that had taken Emma by surprise. Usually they had wardrobes that were identical to each other in every way.

Mia was wearing an obsidian dress with a slit up the side, also paired with black heels, and looked considerably less of a mess than Zoey.

Suddenly, a thought hit Emma, and she couldn't believe she hadn't considered it straight away.

Who was driving the car?

Surely one of the two drunken girls hadn't driven?

That was when it clicked.

The older guys must have been inside the car.

'Are we going?' Mia slurred.

She draped her arm casually around Zoey who was leaning on her for support. Emma was surprised at the sudden breaking of silence. She'd forgotten they planned to get going straight away.

'Sure,' Emma replied and made her way over to the car with the two girls. The feeling of tension crept up on her from earlier, forcing its way under her skin and down her throat.

That was when two guys emerged from the car. They looked to be around twenty-five, or maybe even older than that, but Emma couldn't tell exactly.

One of them had dark green eyes matched with sandy blonde hair that fell into his eyes. Emma assumed this was Mia's boyfriend, Ben, from the way that he was looking at her intently.

The other was sorting out something in his pockets, but when he stood up, Emma could see his profile clearly.

He had chocolate brown hair falling down his back in a ponytail, paired with eyes of the same shade, and displayed just hint of stubble.

'Are we ready to go?' he asked. His voice had a slight huskiness to it.

Both girls were grinning from ear to ear and giggling for no reason.

'Hell yes!' they squealed, getting louder and louder as time went on.

They were obviously in the mood to party until they passed out, but Emma wasn't feeling it.

Perhaps it was just a feeling of awkwardness and tension. Once it wore off, she'd likely be able to enjoy herself.

The cute guy started juggling his keys around in his hands.

Impatience.

Emma knew the signs. Her dad did it all the time.

'What about you?'

He turned his chocolate brown eyes on Emma, surveying her and drinking her in.

She managed a weak smile in response.

'Yeah,' she lied, although at that moment she couldn't think of anything she'd like to do less.

Watching as Zoey, Mia and the blonde guy climbed into the back, she went to climb in too, but brown hair stopped her and led her round to the front of the car. He opened the door.

'After you. No more room in the back,' he explained.

'Thanks.'

She gave him what she hoped was an encouraging smile.

'Joe, by the way,' he introduced, flashing her a warm smile and closing the door as she got into the passenger seat.

Everything was still and silent, except from Zoey and Mia who were giggling uncontrollably in the back.

Emma decided that she would keep her eyes fixed on the window and her surroundings, because she wasn't sure where else to look and what else to do. God, it was uncomfortable.

The driver's door opened, and Joe climbed in, shutting the door behind him and glancing over at her a few times.

He closed the door and started up the engine.

'Seatbelts on, everyone,' he ordered, but his tone was playful.

Emma glanced over at the others, wondering if the worry and tension showed on her face, and hoping it didn't.

Ben met her eyes.

'I've got them, it's fine,' he reassured her, leaning over to ensure their seatbelts were on properly.

'Thanks,' she replied and fixed her own.

As the car moved and the radio played some painfully happy pop stuff, Emma came to a realisation.

Joe was cute.

But Joe was the one that Mia was trying to hook Zoey up with.

She needed to stay out of this one, for sure.

'Do your friends normally get this trashed?' came a voice from next to her, as Joe laughed to himself.

'I wouldn't know,' Emma shrugged.

She needed to be careful when it came to her actions and responses. After all, she hardly knew the guy.

'Why wouldn't you know?'

Emma could hear the interest in his tone as his voice changed completely, and he raised a curious eyebrow at her.

'I was out of college for a year,' she admitted, 'I pulled out for a while.'

'Oh?' His face fell instantly. 'Why?'

He seemed to be concerned. But why would he, or anyone else give a damn?

'Personal issues.'

She shrugged it off as if it was nothing.

'I'm sorry,' he replied softly.

It wasn't long before the car pulled up in front of a building. Emma assumed it was the club.

It looked familiar, which was strange.

'Don't go clubbing often, I'm guessing?' Joe asked, as if he already knew the answer.

Emma simply shrugged, not giving him an answer for a few minutes.

'Am I that easy to read?' she joked, meeting his eyes.

'Nah, I'm just good at these things.' He shrugged nonchalantly as if it was no big deal.

Emma winced as she heard Mia gagging from the backseat. Yep, she was properly drunk.

'Dude, not in my car,' Joe groaned, motioning to Ben to get Mia out of the car, or at least to ensure she was facing the pavement rather than throwing up inside the car.

'Can I help you?' Emma glanced up.

'Yeah, can you grab one of the bottles of water down by your feet?' Joe looked surprised at her offer, but Emma managed to pull one of the freezing bottles out of the packet and pass it over to Mia, who took it in her shaky hands.

It was only then that she remembered that Mia had a fear of puking.

'Drink it slowly,' Ben advised her, rubbing her back in circles and squeezing her hand softly, just as a supportive boyfriend would do.

'This is a new club, then?' Emma asked.

She turned away from the puking scene and looked up at Joe expectantly.

'Yeah, something like that. It got refurbished a few years ago and my friend took over.' Joe shrugged. 'So, we know the owners pretty well.'

'Oh, cool.'

Jesus.

Emma could have said something more interesting. But she didn't have time to think about anything else. All she could think about was Mia throwing up over the pavement.

'We'll give her a few minutes before we get

going,' said Ben. 'Do you think she's going to stop drinking?'

'Probably not.'

Around half an hour later, when Mia had stopped being sick, they woke up Zoey and began to head over to the club to repeat the drinking cycle all over again.

Well, she could guarantee that she wouldn't be getting drunk tonight, but the other two could even end up worse than they had been half an hour ago.

'I'm sorry my girlfriend is an alcoholic,' Ben smirked. Mia rolled her eyes.

'I'm not drunk,' she protested. Her speech was clearer now, but the alcohol was still working on her system.

'Of course not,' he replied sarcastically, hitting her in the arm.

Emma simply smiled at the two of them. They were cute together, but she was pretty certain that Ben's analysis was right – her friend likely did have a drink problem. Or one in the making, at least.

As they made their way over to the glowing beacon that was the club, Emma noticed that it was obviously popular, if the long queue and stern bouncers guarding the place with their lives, were anything to go by.

Looking at them, Emma was reminded of one of her teachers who had believed firmly believed in the benefits of physical punishment in schools.

She shuddered to herself.

Emma was of age, so gaining entry didn't concern her, but her friends weren't old enough yet so there was a good chance they wouldn't be allowed in.

Her anxiety for her friends escalated as they moved further up into the queue. It wasn't that it mattered to her – she'd have been happy to go home that minute – but it was clearly a big deal to them. She cared about that, even if Mia was a dick to her.

The girl at the front of the queue looked to be about fourteen. She had tons of makeup plastered all over her face and was wearing an extremely short outfit. It was so short it caused Emma to get a flash of black lacy underwear when the girl moved.

Emma watched as the bouncer frowned at something the girl said, and it didn't take long before security had grabbed her arms and escorted her to the back of the queue with instructions to leave the area.

'Slut,' she heard Mia mumble under her breath.

'Yeah, because you can talk,' Emma muttered as they moved into the front of the queue.

Now it was their turn. Emma's nerves were creeping back and wrapping around her again as they all hesitantly stepped forwards.

What if they didn't get in?

'Relax.'

Joe leaned over, lips his brushing her ear as he spoke. 'We have a plan.'

Joe and Ben led their small group forward, and it was almost as if they were preparing for heading into battle.

As they reached the front, they approached the bouncers.

'ID?'

One of the bouncers spoke in tones softer and gentler than they'd used on others outside the club.

Soon, and much to Emma's surprise, the bouncers were ushering them inside.

She could have sworn that Joe had said something strange to the bouncers. It sounded almost as if he had said 'We've got another few girls tonight'. But Emma brushed it off and walked inside.

Aventurine was exactly as she expected.

Multi-coloured lights on the walls were searching through the club to find their next victim to cast under the spotlight.

The dancefloor was already completely packed full of sweaty bodies grinding together and dancing to music so loud that it was hard to hear anything else at all.

Emma bit her lip and searched through the crowds to find a space that wasn't so crowded.

There was currently an empty bar. Her eyes locked onto it as if it could save her life.

This place was an introvert's real-life nightmare.

'What's up?' Joe shouted to her over the music, and it was only then that she realised the group had split.

'Emma,' he repeated.

She looked up.

'Sorry, I was just taking everything in.'

'It's alright,'

'What about you?'

'I'm sick of the lovebirds over there.'

He shrugged and ran a hand through his hair.

Emma frowned, following his eyes to see Mia pressed against a wall. Her arms were pinned against it, and an unknown guy was grinding against her. The two were kissing passionately.

Ben was going to be pissed.

Emma's eyes moved back to Joe and her safe place.

'Want a drink?' Joe asked her with a raised eyebrow.

Emma: Experiences

'Only one drink, though.'

Emma's tone was firm and serious. She had said she would only have one alcoholic drink tonight and she meant that. She would only have one drink!

Emma had already learned her lesson from seeing Zoey and Mia stumbling around drunk everywhere and violently throwing up.

But she was happy to have one. After all, it wasn't like she would die or become seriously ill from one little glass of alcohol.

'Okay then, one drink it is.'

Joe smiled at her, and the mischievous twinkle was back in his eyes.

Was he up to something?

Emma wouldn't have put it past him at that moment. She didn't even know him that well, and he could have had anything in his mind or up his sleeve.

'Seriously, one drink.'

Her eyes held an intense, piercing stare as she looked at him, a warning tone clear in her voice.

If he tried anything, she would know instantly.

Tonight, especially she was determined to remain vigilant and sober, especially since she was in a place she didn't know – and surrounded by strangers.

Emma had her own reasons behind hardly ever drinking. The only time that she ever had more than a few drinks was either at birthdays or Christmas: special events where all the family came together to celebrate.

Joe however, looked like he could hold his alcohol extremely well, no matter how large the quantity.

Glancing over at Joe buying the drinks, Emma

paused. They still needed to find a seat, but there were booths in the far corner that didn't look quite as packed as everywhere else.

Ignorant about bars and clubs, Emma stood by Joe's side and watched the various lights from the ceiling as they searched through the crowd for their next victims to bathe in colour.

Cyan blue lights suddenly flashed into her eyes which fell back onto a now hot-pink Joe. She giggled.

'You look really girly.'

Joe did a mock bow.

'And you look very blue.'

As people gathered and a crowd was formed, Joe held on to Emma's hand tightly as if to comfort her. It was just what she needed, but how did he know that Emma was slightly claustrophobic and hated crowds?

Strange.

Emma brushed it off as simple coincidence. She had no idea where Ben, Zoey and Mia had got to, but she decided they were probably together or busy elsewhere.

'What do you want to drink?' Joe shouted over the music, which seemed to be getting louder every few minutes.

'Surprise me!' Emma shouted back in response.

Emma thought she saw Joe wince which just confirmed her suspicions about the music's volume.

'Okay.' He shot her a mischievous grin and sauntered off to the bar, but as she watched Joe walk away, her heart started pounding. She could almost hear it, even over the music.

But it didn't take long for him to get served, and soon he was pushing through the crowd again.

Noticing that he was heading towards one of the booths in the far corner, she followed, pushing through the crowds herself, holding her breath till she was free of them.

Letting out a breath, she smiled.

She'd made it out unscathed.

She'd done it.

Allowing herself to feel proud, she slid into a seat next to Joe. The tray, plus drinks and Joe's wallet were perched on the table.

'Sorry.'

He finally spoke up after catching his breath.

'I spilt the drinks a bit, but I'm sure they taste alright.'

To confirm this, he took a gulp of his own drink and gave a thumbs up, seeming to shudder at the strength of it.

Emma laughed.

'I know you spilt the drinks; I saw you trip, and you can't really hide the evidence that's right there on the tray.'

'I never did that!'

Emma smirked and rolled her eyes.

'The drinks taste fine though,' he added with a stupid grin on his face.

'This one is yours.'

He winked at her, taking the large bottle and glass and sliding them over to her.

The glass held huge clumps of ice at the bottom which looked as if they were clinging onto the glass for dear life. Emma unscrewed the top of the bottle and winced as she cut her finger.

It was a small jagged cut, and nothing major.

She filled her glass to the brim and peered into the contents, swirling the transparent liquid around with her free hand.

It reminded her slightly of blood.

Her mind automatically took her to a place where the characters drunk blood, or something else that had been drugged or spiked.

But this wasn't a horror film.

This was real life. And that kind of thing didn't happen in real life.

Joe finally explained: 'It is basically flavoured and diluted vodka'.

'Oh,' was all she could say in response.

See?

It wasn't blood.

When Emma finally took a sip, the drink had a weird taste - at first quite dry, then after a few minutes a combination of flavours hit her. The sweetness increased after a while and there was a small taste of berries that emerged from each gulp.

It was hard to decide if she was enjoying it or not. But maybe enjoyment wasn't the point. Most people only drunk alcohol in order to get drunk.

'Do you drink a lot then?'

'Sometimes. It really just depends on where I am, I guess,' he replied, shrugging. 'What about you?'

'Not much, honestly. But you knew that already,' Emma pointed out, looking down into the now empty depths of her glass.

'Do you know where the toilets are?' Emma asked. Joe paused for a few seconds, as if there was something else going on.

What was that about?

'Um...' He trailed off, stood up and ran his hand through his hair, as if in frustrated contemplation. She could see his eyes scanning over the top of the dancing and drinking crowd.

'Over there,' he replied suddenly, almost as

eruptive as if he'd had a eureka moment. There was something nervy about his tone. And something else...

It seemed to be fear.

'Okay, I'll be a few minutes,' said Emma and, keeping her voice and attitude casual, she pushed through the manic crowd, trying to reach the glowing neon pink Ladies sign.

She couldn't put her finger on it, but something felt odd. If there was anything going on with Joe, she didn't want to give away that she knew something was wrong.

Eventually reaching the toilets, she pushed the door open and headed in, Bizarrely, the toilets were empty. Thank goodness. She could take a breath and calm herself.

It was then that she heard footsteps and ducked into a toilet stall.

'We know you're in there.'

It was Zoey, but she didn't sound like the normal Zoey. She was harsh. Aggressive. Drunk.

'Get the fuck out of there!' she yelled, slurring drunkenly.

Nervously, Emma pushed the stall door open, and watched as it swung with a creak. She hadn't realised till that moment that her hands were shaking.

'You bitch,' Zoey growled, slapping Emma hard across the face which caused Emma to stumble back slightly into the stall.

'What did I do?' Emma asked, genuinely confused. There was no way she'd ever offend Zoey on purpose.

'You stole Joe away from me!' Zoey yelled as previously giddy girls just opening the door to the toilets, froze at the door. Watching and waiting for something to happen.

Emma took a deep breath and willed her

hands to stop shaking.

'I don't know what you're talking about.'

There was anger in Zoey's eyes as she took a few steps forward.

'Sure, you don't.'

Zoey glared.

Emma looked over to Mia for help, but even she was avoiding her gaze.

'We were just talking. I swear we were.'

Emma put her hands up in objection, and to defend herself. Her eyes flickered over to the door and to their growing audience.

In all the time they'd been friends, Emma had never seen Zoey like this. She had read that alcohol changes people, but never seen such an obvious and frightening change as this in person.

'He bought you a drink.'

Zoey's voice was dripping with accusation and malice.

'It was only a drink.'

A bitter laugh came from Zoey.

'Just a drink…'

Zoey paused for a few moments before continuing with a comment that came from nowhere.

'You obviously like him.'

'I only met him for five minutes!'

With that, Emma ran out of the toilets, narrowly avoiding Zoey's attempted lunge at her.

Toilets left behind; Emma made a move towards the booth that Joe had claimed for them. Her brain was pounding against her skull.

Getting closer to Joe, the dizziness began to set in.

'I've got her,' was the last thing she heard before darkness wrapped itself around her, the crowds disappeared from her consciousness, and everything stopped.

The Castle: Captive

When she awoke from her rough sleep, she found herself tangled up in blood red sheets, making her legs look like they were smothered in claret and silhouetted against the canopy hanging freely from her bed.

Or was she a goddess lounging decadently for a studio photograph?

The sting of failure twisted around her like the sheets that trapped her. Of course, the king wouldn't let her leave now – not when he needed his prize possession the most.

It was when she heard the two sharp taps at the door that her heart leapt into her throat. She'd be in all sorts of trouble now. She didn't even want to think about how much danger she would be in.

Last time was bad enough.

Hearing the door creak open, her eyes instantly shot open and her body became alert despite her apparent weakness. She didn't know how willing her body would be to protect itself when it was in this state, but she was damn well going to try.

Her whole demeanour relaxed when she saw that it was only her best friend, Michael. Unfortunately, he was of a much lower rank than her and the king didn't exactly like them hanging around each other.

Even so, he was the only person in the castle that she could truly trust - without a single doubt in her mind.

'My lady.'

Michael bowed to her and shut the door behind him as he slid into the room. A silver tray was propped up at her bedside table. On the tray were a goblet of liquid that she didn't recognise, a glass of water and a large plate of food.

'I thought I told you never to call me that again,' Emma grinned at him.

He just shrugged, 'Appearances.' His reply came as if it explained everything.

'Understandable,' Emma replied, smiling slightly. 'What's up?'

Her eyes searched Michael's face for answers as his expression darkened and he let out a heavy sigh.

'I'm sorry about what happened to you. I didn't do anything to stop it.'

Emma just cast her eyes to the floor, and her skin turned a sickly pale colour again.

'I don't want to talk about it,' she whispered.

'The king told me to get you to drink that.'

Michael gestured towards the glass.

'You don't have to, though. It's a sleeping draught.'

'Of course,' she muttered.

Michael turned away slowly.

'Well, I'll let you get some sleep then.'

She decided not to question why the king would give her a sleeping draught.

'Michael?'

'Yeah?'

'Thank you.'

'For what?'

Michael peeked up at her curiously from his position by the door.

'Being a friend.'

Emma's fingers played with her bedcovers absentmindedly as she gave him a warm and reassuring smile. He returned it with the slightest hint of a blush as he gave a small bow and disappeared from the room as quickly as he had come in.

As soon as Michael left, Emma frantically searched around in her covers for the notebook that she normally kept under her bed. Pulling it out from under her bed sheets, she hesitated.

Why was it here and not under her bed like normal?

She shrugged it off, assuming she'd probably forgotten to put it back. However, she needed to be far more careful.

If Cole found a notebook full of ideas that were meant to be used to kill him, she would be in deep trouble.

Emma: Captive

Every time she tried to move, a sharp pain ran from the back of her head and all the way down the rest of her body. It was too much, so she stopped moving and tried to use her eyes to salvage details of the scene in front and around of her.

When her eyes adjusted, she could make out a figure, and eventually realised that the figure was in front of a steering wheel.

A car?

Was she in a car?

Emma couldn't remember even stepping into a vehicle, so why was she here with this random person? Nothing made any sense.

A wave of exhaustion kicked at her again impatiently, waiting and gnawing inside of her to come out and play.

Remaining still and silent, she looked over at the figure again. She couldn't see much as his body and face were all covered with a black hoodie. She saw the figure move a little. She must pretend she was still disorientated.

Shortly after, she heard the driver door slam shut and footsteps outside. She swallowed down her panic when the car door on her side opened and the figure from behind emerged out of the shadows.

'Go back to sleep,' the husky voice whispered as he tilted her neck to the side and injected something into her neck with a long needle and syringe.

Emma's head lolled to one side and everything become silent inside it again.

When Emma's eyes snapped open, all of her previous erratic thoughts returned to her restless mind.

Questions came to her almost instantly, but there were none that she could answer.

Sharp stings and aches pulsated through her body like a steady beat of a drum.

At least she could still feel.

Her vision was blurry, and she couldn't make out much, but she knew from the lights fading in and out that something was wrong - either with her or with the room.

She struggled to look down at her body, and as the pain in her neck increased, she realised that she was completely right.

Ropes bound her wrists together and also to the chair that she was sitting in. No wonder she could barely move. Her captor obviously wanted her helpless and vulnerable.

Suddenly, she heard heavy footsteps from outside the room she was in, along with raised voices and slamming doors.

That didn't make her feel any less anxious.

Emma was completely on her own, and inevitably, she didn't know how long she would last.

The first figure to storm into the room caught and held her attention instantly. He would tower over her even if she wasn't forced to be sitting down. His hair was a dark shade of brown, his fringe was slicked back whilst the rest of his long hair had been left to tumble down his shoulders. The most unusual thing about this man was his eyes which were a light shade of grey. Under any other circumstance, Emma probably would have found him attractive.

She tore her eyes away from his cloudy grey orbs and looked towards the second person who had entered and stood beside him.

This one wore a hoodie, and even though his

face was obscured, he seemed familiar to her somehow.

As if she knew him.

It was deathly silent in the room and Emma knew instinctively not to make any noise that would give away that she was awake and conscious.

As long as they weren't looking over at her and she was silent, the men wouldn't take any notice.

Sighs of relief from the two men broke the silence.

Emma kept trying to remember how she got here but her mind kept coming up blank. It was almost like there was blockage that prevented her from tapping into the past few hours.

'Is she awake?' a deep voice asked. Emma tried to trace the accent, but her brain was a mess and she couldn't think straight.

As she heard footsteps heading toward her, she closed her eyes instantly.

It wasn't that hard to do when her body wanted desperately to shut down.

She could imagine dark eyes raking down her entire body and she felt herself shudder involuntarily. That one movement could have cost her everything.

'She's asleep.'

Another voice. This time it was one that she could place.

Joe.

Had he had this intention all along? Was Joe the one who had arranged all of this?

None of this made any sense.

She wanted to scream at him, yell at him, cry or do anything to gain his attention.

But she didn't.

Who knew what would happen if they found out that she was awake?

Taking a deep breath and making sure that the two men had left completely, she opened her eyes and moved to sit up so that she could take in her location.

Well, what she could see of it anyway.

Emma noticed that there was a small light swinging from the ceiling, with a fraying lead that looked as if it could break anytime soon. The glow it gave off was eerie, but at least the room was lit. She wouldn't have been able to cope with darkness, especially with the room slipping in and out of focus.

A glossy black desk was pressed up against the wall closest to the door, and a variety of tools were placed neatly across it, in some kind of order that Emma couldn't figure out.

So - that told her that her captor was obsessive about cleaning and also had an interest in DIY and possibly construction. She made a mental note to remember this for later.

Turning to her side and earning another stab of pain for defying her body, she noticed for the first time, a white trolley. Emma recognised a few of the medical items on it, but what caught her attention most were the three syringes in a metal container. On was already filled with a murky liquid that was a mixture of brown and green. Were these syringes intended for her? And what were the contents of that dark orange folder on one of the lower levels of the trolley. She began to reach for it, but suddenly the door swung open, the creaking noise making the hairs on the back of her neck stand up.

'Oh look. Sleeping Beauty is awake,' he said, his tone patronising and cold.

She could see him clearly now. He was a man who was probably about thirty, perhaps younger.

'What am I doing here?' Emma asked as he knelt in front of her, like he was preparing to speak to a child.

Bastard.

'You wouldn't like the answer... besides, we're going to have a lot of fun together.'

He got up and paced around her chair with a smile.

The sadistic expression caused Emma to struggle and pull at her restraints so hard that she was certain that she was bleeding.

She screamed in pain and the man placed a finger to her lip.

'Ssh. That will only drain your energy, Emma.' A knowing smile crept onto his face.

Against his advice, she continued to struggle which only made her muscles ache until it was unbearable.

He leaned over and whispered in her ear 'You're not playing by the rules, Emma' before slapping her hard across the face.

Emma recoiled, the sharp slap hurt like hell, but not as much as her muscles currently.

'I can't talk to you when you're like this. How unfortunate, I wanted to get to know you better,' He sighed dramatically, picking up the syringe beside her filled with the murky liquid.

'What the hell is that?'

Her usual calm voice betrayed her instantly, making her sound panicked and desperate.

'Something that will make you more agreeable for later,' he smirked.

Later?

Grabbing her arm roughly, he plunged the needle attached to the syringe in and grinned as the liquid travelled down the syringe and into her veins.

Emma became a victim of the darkness again.

Cole

Placing Emma in a bed as she slept, a smile crept up slowly onto Cole's face.

Cole belonged in the shadows - his family had made certain of that.

Hopefully, when Emma woke up in around three hours, she would be a lot more docile.

Cole got up from his stool and headed over to the desk, opening one of the drawers and retrieving his stack of photographs. He had to dispose of them. Emma would never understand if she saw them.

Pulling out his lighter from his pocket, he let the photos burn and watched as they gave off a small source of light in the darkest room of the house.

Those photos were memories that he didn't need to be reminded of in this new reality.

The mother that killed herself because of his father's abuse – to both of them, not just her.

Putting them both behind him and starting over was important. Even his therapist had agreed with him. He had told Cole that the past was the past and that he needed to let go. That was why he was doing this now.

Emma would be safer here than she would be at home. He would give her everything she would ever need to survive.

She was all he needed.

Cole would start a new family.

A family without problems.

A family that would run smoothly.

He wouldn't be his father.

Not this time.

The Castle: The Dress

Emma eventually managed to wake up and get out of bed. She had refused to take the sleeping draft and came to the realisation that it would need to be disposed of, so the king didn't know she hadn't taken it.

Dispose of it down the sink perhaps?

This was a good suggestion from inside her head - for once.

Getting up and darting into the bathroom with the sleeping draught, she ignored her body's tremendous pain and struggled to pour all of the contents of the large glass into the sink, turning on the taps so it washed down quickly.

Freezing as there came a few sharp taps on the door, she broke out of her trance and ran back into the bedroom. She set the glass back on her tray, and waited for the moment when the person would walk in. Nothing.

She got herself from the bed and opened the door slowly. Standing there were two guards clad in silver armour, marked with the tell-tale red and black crest of the kingdom.

'Miss Winters?' one of them asked in a gruff voice.

Joseph.

He was the one who hit the hardest and left most of the bruises on her body, laughing as he did so.

'Yes?' Emma asked, trying not to show any facial expressions that might get her hit.

'King Cole would like to see you, immediately,' he replied, looking at her in a way that made her feel extremely uncomfortable and self-conscious. Knowing that she couldn't refuse or say no in this situation, she simply nodded in agreement.

'May I have a few minutes to dress?' She gave a gesture to her clothes that looked inappropriate, or even indecent for a meeting with the king. She received a curt nod from Joseph, and as soon as they left, she began an examination of her wardrobe.

In the end she selected a darkened violet coloured dress that was made from silk and chiffon matched with sheer sleeves. Emma wondered what he would make her do this time.

Slipping her small feet into heeled shoes of the same colour, she stumbled over to the door, testing her stability in the unaccustomed heels. Emma mainly used objects around her to lean on as she stumbled and tripped her way over to the door.

'Are you ready now?' Joseph asked her, looking at her way longer than was strictly necessary. In response, Emma inclined her head and followed both guards down the corridor, decorated with portraits of Cole. These were completely and utterly self-absorbing, and every one was the same as she remembered. But the coal-black double doors in front of them were never the same. They decided the fate of poor unfortunates in seconds.

Reaching the great hall, she proceeded to allow the guards to lead her in and ignored the nervous feelings infecting all parts of her body and almost closing up her throat. As they neared Cole's throne, she noticed a few members of the court tense up. She would be the spectacle and the court's main entertainment.

Cole smirked at her, and she knew that this

wasn't going to end well. After all, Emma refused to follow him and accept him as her king.

She watched as he rose from his throne suddenly and dramatically.

'Emma,' he said, his eyes focused entirely on her.

'Cole,' she spat in a bitter tone, glaring.

Cole swirled round to look at the court and the guards.

'You can all leave now.'

His tone held ice within it, which didn't reassure her at all.

They were soon alone, and he could do anything he wanted.

'So,' he began coldly. Despite the cold, anger was evident in his voice.

Emma swallowed back panic. Was he going to hit her now?

'You escaped, but it won't happen again.'

Emma stayed quiet.

Cole growled at her, eyes blazing.

'Remember, you do have a voice.'

That was when he started pacing.

'That won't happen again,' Emma's voice trembled in terror.

'No, it won't,' he smirked, running a possessive hand over her flesh, which sent shivers down her back and spine.

'You don't belong to anyone else. I can do whatever I want to you and whatever I want with your life.'

He pushed her down onto her knees and snarled at her.

'Now,' he started, standing over her. 'Tell me that you're sorry and it will never happen again.'

'I'm sorry. It won't happen again,' Emma repeated in a whisper.

Emma gave herself a gentle reminder that she had to do everything she was told in order to survive. Cole smirked, tilting Emma's chin up with his forefinger and stroking her cheek softly with his thumb.

Emma looked up at him obediently.

'Do you know what?' Cole asked her, moving down to her level yet still towering over her.

'What, s-sire?'

She had to restrain herself from pulling back from him, and especially from the evil glint in his eyes.

Cole smiled and leaned in close to her ear.

'I don't believe you.'

He delivered a kick to her ribs as he whispered the words.

Emma let out a bloodcurdling scream.

'What's wrong, Emma? Chest pain?'

Emma gritted her teeth in pain and began to rise from the floor.

'Did I say you could get up?'

She sank back down.

'Much better,' he responded in praise.

Cole chuckled.

'You'd better go and get ready for the masquerade tonight, I expect to see you there,' he grinned. 'Wear the outfit on your bed,'

As she struggled up and headed to the door, she heard him call her back.

'Oh, and Emma? Be careful, I wouldn't want you to get hurt.'

Cole gave her a smug smile.

As soon as she had left the great hall behind, she slumped against a wall and pulled her knees up to her chest for some slight comfort. But the comfort wasn't to be found.

'Emma?' came Michael's voice. 'My lady?' he asked again, even more concerned than before.

Emma simply shook her head, not wanting to say anything.

She steadily got up onto her feet, trying to ignore the pain demanding her attention like a small child.

'Somewhere else.'

Emma's voice was quieter than normal. She couldn't risk anything right now. Impulsively, she grabbed Michael's arm and pulled him into an empty room that she knew hardly ever got used.

'We can talk now.'

'What happened?'

'I think he broke a few of my ribs,' Emma admitted, finally allowing herself to acknowledge the pain.

'The king?'

Michael ran a hand through his hair nervously.

'You have to tell someone!'

'As much as I want to, I can't.'

Emma gave a heavy sigh.

Michael also sighed in response.

'At least let me get you to a physician,'

'He'd find out,' Emma whispered.

'It's better than nothing.'

'Okay, fine, but we need to think of a cover story to explain the injuries.'

Michael led her through the never-ending hallways.

Emma: Vulnerable

As soon as Emma opened her eyes, she felt as if her mind had hit a wall of exhaustion. She couldn't think straight.

Forcing herself up and out of bed, she was shocked and relieved that she seemed to be back in her bedroom.

Confusion hit her like a brick.

Was this all an illusion or a trick of the mind?

She had been wrapped in her own duvet – the one that her mother had bought for her. And all the furniture in the room was the same.

Her pillows were scattered around the floor, yet again.

Emma must have lashed out in her sleep - she was always doing that.

Noticing a brush on her bedside table, she picked it up and ran it through her tangled, messy hair.

She should probably get up and get dressed to head into college. She should probably pick an outfit to wear for the day.

That was when a door opened, and she watched as a figure walked in.

'Morning.'

He gave her a sneering smile.

'I think we can talk now, don't you?'

Emma's spirit fell in an instant, and bile rose up her throat as everything crashed and burned inside her mind.

She wasn't safe anymore.

Taking a deep breath in as her captor approached her, Emma instinctively began to consider the most important thing of all – self-protection.

Jumping back and instinctively running to her

bed, she sat down and drew her knees up to her chin like a small child might if faced with unimaginable danger. And even in this position she could feel her body shaking.

Eyeing the man cautiously, Emma watched as he approached the bed, placed a tray in front of her and walked over to the wardrobe, clearly searching for something.

The tray in front of her held a large plate of food and a steaming mug of liquid, likely coffee or tea.

Bang. Something hit the floor with a light thud and she instantly recoiled from the noise.

When she realised that it was just a foldable chair, her cheeks turned a dark pink as she tried to calm her heart rate down.

The chair was positioned opposite her end of the bed and she watched the space with hawk eyes, just waiting for any sudden unanticipated movement.

'I didn't know whether you took tea or coffee, so I made a bit of a guess.'

He leaned back in the chair, observing her.

Emma stayed quiet, till she eventually found enough courage to talk.

'I prefer tea to coffee.'

'That's what I thought.' A brief smile appeared on his face but disappeared just as quickly as it had come.

Emma dealt with the awkward silence by toying with her duvet cover. Peering up at her captor, she noticed the purple circles under his eyes.

He looked exhausted, but a glance down at her own wrists was enough to revoke any sympathy that she felt for him. They were still a dull red colour, stained with the aftermath of yesterday.

They ached too, reminding her constantly of

what she'd been through.

Yes, this man was the reason why she was here in the first place.

Emma picked up the mug of tea and sipped it slightly, not realising how thirsty she was. But she was going to force herself to take it slow, however dry her throat was.

What exactly should she say to him?

It wasn't like they could just have a relaxed chat about the weather.

'Did you sleep well?'

Emma frowned for a few moments, initially taken aback as she didn't even remember having slept, though she must have done as she felt rested and awake.

'Yes,' she replied quietly. She picked up the cutlery from the tray and began to eat.

The background noise of the clock ticking was the only thing breaking the silence between them.

It didn't break the tension.

'You must be wondering why you're here?'

It was a statement that made Emma's head snap up. The cutlery she was holding clattered back onto the tray and her undivided attention was given to her captor.

'Maybe,' Emma admitted.

He had her right where he wanted her to be.

'I need you to do me a few favours,' he stated, his attention suddenly directed entirely towards Emma. His eyes fixated on her.

'Nothing serious, don't worry,' he added, his voice eerily calm.

Emma watched as her captor got up, heading towards her. She began to panic. What was he going to do?

He leaned over and picked up her tray, and

now empty plate and mug.

Emma exhaled and relaxed.

He wasn't going to hurt her after all.

Not yet.

He turned to leave, then swirled back round to face Emma and smiled: 'If you do the favours I ask of you, I'll allow you to eat and drink.'

Emma would have made some response, but he was already gone.

She looked around the room blankly for a moment, then down at her dirty, crumpled clothes.

Would he bring her something new to wear?

Deciding to consult the wardrobe, just in case it held something she could use, she got up off the bed and walked over.

Opening it slowly, she fully expected something to fall out of the wardrobe and land on top of her. Maybe she was just being paranoid.

Instead, inside that wardrobe, she simply saw all sorts of clothes. They were mainly bright colours but included a multitude of trousers, skirts, tops and dresses.

No shoes though.

Strange.

Had other people stayed here before her?

A note fluttered out from the top of the wardrobe as she picked an outfit and placed it on the bed.

Picking up the note and reading it, she made out the words

It was too much.
I couldn't take it anymore.
I'm sorry.
Maisie

Why did that name sound so familiar?

Suddenly she knew the priority was to find out what happened to this girl before it happened to her.

Rushing over to the window, she frantically tried to open it.

Of course, you needed a key.

Clever.

She needed to find a way out.

The Castle

Having Michael's help in walking made Emma instantly feel a lot more supported. She was pretty sure that she was unintentionally putting all her body weight onto him to keep herself vaguely stable. The pain from her ribs increased until she felt as if they were on fire, and the flames were pulsating all the way through her body.

'We'll rest when we get closer. Okay?' Michael's voice was soothing, but he made her push on through the pain till they arrived, which was exactly what Emma would have told him to do. If they did stop, then Cole could find them and who knew what would happen then?

Meanwhile, Emma was trying to fight against the pain with as much force as she could, even if it was exhausting her in the process.

Soon they arrived in the lower town, where rain fell from the sky like crystallised glass tears. There was hardly anyone in town. Emma assumed they were all locked up safely in their homes - and she couldn't blame them. Normally people would be out playing and working, but rain like this would keep anyone indoors.

Emma was so transfixed by the town that she didn't realise that Michael was chatting away to her. It had even distracted her from the pain circulating around her ribs.

'Emma? Are you okay?' Michael's voice faded back in suddenly.

'Yeah, I was just thinking.' Emma shrugged.

'What about?'

There was a sudden change in his voice that she didn't recognise.

'It's quiet,' she stated simply, looking around to prove her point.

'Yeah, I noticed that too.'

Michael looked around and frowned slightly. Was he holding something back from her?

It only took a few minutes until they were standing in front of a small building that looked as if it had only recently been built. A cloud of anxiety and guilt plagued her as she headed into the physician's quarters, leaning on Michael for essential support.

'My lady.'

The physician bowed to her.

Emma had forgotten his name, but it wasn't her fault - she hardly ventured down here much.

His dark blue eyes widened as he assessed her appearance.

'My lady? Are you unwell?'

There was clear concern in his voice.

Emma opened her mouth to speak but Michael cut in.

'I'm pretty sure she has a few fractured ribs,' he explained. 'Quite a few bruises.'

The physician paused. 'How did this happen?' he asked.

Michael shot Emma a nervous glance which she hoped the physician hadn't seen.

'I fell down the stairs.'

She lied easily and he nodded in response. She had forgotten how easy it could be to tell an untruth.

'I may have something that can help with that.'

The physician immediately began searching

his cupboards, producing a set of vials containing a lemon-yellow liquid.

'Have you seen a basket anywhere?' he asked suddenly, frantically scanning around the room.

'This?' Michael asked with a raised eyebrow as he effortlessly produced a basket from under the desk.

'Yes.'

He slipped the vials into the basket carefully.

'Take one every night until the pain ceases. If f you need more, come back to see me.'

Emma took the basket and headed to the door with Michael.

'Oh, and my lady?'

Emma's eyes looked over curiously.

'Try not to fall down the stairs again.'

He knew what had happened. She knew he did.

Emma: Trapped

Emma was struggling to come up with any ideas about how she would get out of the room.

Any thoughts that did waft into her consciousness would have been too easy for him to figure out. She had to try and think 'out of the box' for once, and that would be easier said than done.

It was hard to think about anything under these circumstances.

Surely there must be something here she could do to entertain herself while she he was out?

That was when her search began.

Emma began with the drawers. After opening each in turn, she found a colouring book with a pack of pens still in the packaging. She also discovered a slightly ripped pack of playing cards. The box that contained them was decaying slowly but the cards looked perfectly fine.

Emma scavenged around for anything else that she could find, but there was nothing.

But Emma had a feeling deep inside of her that boredom wouldn't be the only feeling that she would have to deal with over the coming days.

Beth: The Beginnings

Beth stared into space, pondering how things were and how they had been. All potential focus on the television and the news had been abandoned as her thoughts kicked in and came to life.

One of her best and oldest friends had gone missing and she felt sick to her stomach as she twirled a strand of dirty blonde hair around her finger, picking up the mug next to her and taking a slow sip.

Perhaps if she'd done something differently and maybe sent her a message earlier, Emma might not have disappeared. Despite all the arguments they used to have, she did still care about her.

But they'd had one argument too many, the friendship began to disappear, and they stopped talking for a while. Beth had failed Emma and then had tried to get back in contact too late. What she should have done was prevented any arguments in the first place.

Beth assumed that Emma had simply moved on now she was at college. She would have had a whole new group of friends and a whole different life - without her in it. But this was something that nobody would have expected.

Suddenly something on the television caught her attention. Grabbing her remote and turning the volume up higher, she listened to the news report about Emma with careful concentration. The news report stated that she was missing. It seemed that everyone assumed she was just a teenage runaway.

But Beth knew different. Emma wasn't the type to run away from her problems.

And things were even worse because of all the news stories. Recent reports had been all about a maniac on the loose – a man who police were unable to catch. The stories told horrors of how most of his victims died with burn marks etched across their skin. Those who survived were sent to hospital for long-term psychological treatment.

Whipping her head around to the side, she saw a flash of light out of the corner of her eye.

What was it?

Letting her erratic heart beat calm down, she realised that it was only her phone.

It was a text from Michael. She sighed. He was starting to get irritating, but not to the point that Beth didn't want to talk to him.

She had never been so close to Michael. It had only really started to become close when Emma disappeared. He used to follow Emma around like a lost puppy, but he had promised Beth that he would help in the task of finding her.

'Fancy a meet-up?' the text read. Emma winced.

Now?

She hadn't even had a chance to wake up properly.

Beth assumed he wanted her company because of his coursework. He constantly had problems with it, but luckily, she knew the subject, and could help.

That was the cost. She helped him with his coursework, and he helped her with finding out more about Emma's disappearance.

'Where?'

She headed upstairs, taking her phone along with her. She had to get ready just in case the response to her text came through quickly.

Emma: Masquerade

Four hours had passed since Emma's captor had come into her bedroom.

Hearing the door unlock again, she froze and pushed aside the colouring book and pencils as her captor strode in, face completely blank.

Emma watched as his eyes scanned her up and down. They then left her body and flitted towards the colouring book that she had cast aside.

'You've been drawing,' he observed, walking over to her bedside and picking the book up. 'It looks nice.'

Casually, he threw the colouring book down on the bed, and sat down next to her.

'I'm holding a masquerade ball party tonight.'

He held up three elaborate and fancy dresses in front of him for her to view.

There wasn't much choice, and she definitely wasn't in the mood for a party.

'First, we need to change your appearance a bit.' He threw her a smirk.

What?

She didn't have time to respond as he stroked at her hair and quickly pulled her arm, dragging her into the bathroom.

He grabbed a towel from the side of the porcelain bath and threw it on the floor.

'Kneel down on the towel,' he ordered.

There was no option other than obedience.

For now, she had to do what he asked of her. It was the only thing that would keep her safe. She didn't even dare look up just in case he took it as a challenge.

Emma heard him open a packet of something and soon afterwards felt him rubbing something in her hair, lathering up whatever it was. Shampoo perhaps?

Then the smell hit her.

Hair dye.

He really was changing her appearance.

Panic ran through her veins. How the hell was anyone going to find her now, or even believe her when she did escape and tell them who she was?

Her captor watched as the dye settled into her hair.

'Stay still, till I tell you otherwise,' he ordered, leaving the room.

She had little other choice.

Half an hour later, he returned. At least, she thought it was about that time. She'd been counting down within her head, hoping that the time would pass quickly.

'Lean over the bath,' he instructed.

'Why are you doing this?' she whispered.

Silence.

She looked up at him and he pushed her body forward so that her head and neck were bent over the white, porcelain bath.

She heard his heavy sigh as he tested the water, turning the taps to make sure that it was hot enough.

Watching the dye trickle into the bath, Emma realised her hair had been transformed to a coal black shade.

Why black?

He could have selected any other colour.

Emma went silent and just simply watched as the colour disappeared down the drain.

It took a few minutes to wash out completely, and then her hair was draped and covered in a scarlet towel.

She was taken into the room. She assumed it was where she'd be staying for however long she was his prisoner.

Her bedroom.

But it didn't feel like her room anymore.

Especially not with this new hair.

Her captor sat behind her and produced something from his pocket that glittered in the few strands of light piercing the room.

As he began to cut, she watched as her wet hair fell to the floor and she held back tears as the last physical echoes of the person she used to be faded away before her eyes.

After what seemed like an eternity of cutting her hair, the man stepped back to examine his creation.

Making a curt noise of approval, he allowed Emma to get up. He left the room again, just briefly.

She dreaded seeing the person she'd become and glanced up slowly, scared in case there was a mirror nearby. The first thing she saw were the three dresses on hangers draped next to where she was sitting.

He pushed his head through the door.

'Pick a dress and wear one.'

He locked her door and disappeared.

Emma glanced over the first dress. It had a complete cut-out back; it was in fire engine red and completely sleeveless. It wouldn't give her much flexibility, but overall it looked like the most elegant option.

Emma peered over at the next dress - dark blue with long see-through sleeves. The body was made completely of lace – innocent and floaty.

The final dress choice was turquoise and

looked simpler and more casual than the other two. It was sleeveless with white polka dots and a brown belt. It was almost a weird version of a skater dress.

Emma made her selection choice and hung it up on the wardrobe door so it wouldn't get creased or damaged.

Not one of the dresses was anything at all like something she'd usually wear.

She put the other dresses to the side and let her thoughts drift away. What was going to happen tonight? Why hold a party? Who was the girl who wrote the note? And, could she have a proper talk with him if she behaved herself at the party?

She ran her hands through her hair in complete frustration. There was only one way to calm down. She was going to try and get some sleep. Once her head hit the pillow, it was easy enough.

The Castle

Emma made her way to her chambers quickly with Michael's help. She didn't care that maids and servants were watching. They could all gossip if they wanted - idle gossip didn't bother her anymore.

It was eerily quiet when she stepped back inside her chambers, and the only thing that Emma could hear were her own footsteps. Looking on her bed, she found the garment that Cole had told her she was supposed to wear for that evening's ball.

Unlike her usual violet-blue shades, this dress was sleeveless and in a striking blood-red colour. Just looking at it made Emma feel a little bit uncomfortable. When she turned, she saw Cole standing like a statue on the other side of the room.

'S-sire?'

A nervous stutter came from her mouth, which was nothing like the firm way she spoke to him in her head. Fortunately, she gained a little strength from the dulled pain, owing to the contents of one of the physician's vials. Cole glared at her.

'The dress is suitable for tonight?' A question.

'Yes, sire,' she responded, her voice slightly stronger when she saw he was smiling.

'I assume you remember our agreement?'

'Yes,' Emma murmured in response.

'Good.'

His curt response ended their conversation and he turned on his heel and left the room. Emma stared after him then decided to run a bath.

Emma: Talking Back

Emma hadn't even realised she'd successfully fallen asleep, till her captor yelled at her to wake up.

'I'm up!' she snapped, and soon realised her mistake.

'Did you just talk back to me?'

'No,' she lied, avoiding his eyes completely.

That was when she felt it.

The slap came across her face. It stung like hell.

He looked her over and sighed in mock disappointment, tutting at her and shaking his head.

'To think I was going to let you eat tonight.'

As if reading his mind, her stomach betrayed her by letting out a loud rumble.

She hadn't eaten much since arriving here, and the days had just blurred together endlessly.

He laughed in her face.

'Poor darling. Hungry, are you? Maybe next time you should think before talking back to me, sweetheart.'

Beth: College

As was her habit, Beth checked the weather before deciding what to wear. Once she got her outfit together, she dressed slowly.

Her outfit consisted of a loose ocean blue tank top paired with coal black leggings and thigh-high boots of the same shade. Turning around to examine her top from the side, she noticed her top was quite baggy – but not so baggy that it looked like a dress.

At least she still had room to breathe and move around in this outfit without any constrictions. That led to thoughts of Emma. As everything did.

In the back of her mind, Beth knew that the police could release information about her friend at any time, and for some odd reason she preferred to be at home as and when that happened.

Why would she want to be out with other people doing them favours when the main person she really needed to help was Emma.

Maybe their friendship could go back to normal when this was all over. But then again, maybe Emma would come out of it a completely different person.

Everyone said the same. Things didn't stay the same. Time didn't stop. Relationships would always change.

Grabbing one of the many bags hanging on her wardrobe door, she packed it quickly. Checking her phone battery percentage, she was relieved that it was fully charged. With a sigh of satisfaction, she slipped it into her coat pocket.

No sooner had she put it in the pocket, and pulled the coat on, the phone began buzzing and vibrating against the material. It was a reply from Michael that confirmed the normal meeting place would be fine.

Beth headed out of the front door and walked down the street, turning a corner to head into town. The music now blaring into her ears was from the same playlist she must have been listening to while she fell asleep.

She fired off another text to say that she was on her way before shoving her phone back into her pocket and enjoying the music.

Beth had chosen to start college for a reason. A change.

But not everything can change. It seemed she was being dragged back to the place she'd once been when her and Emma were constantly arguing. But she didn't want those memories anymore.

Soon she found herself in the town centre – the area where most of the decent shops were. She was surprised at how empty the town was – unusually empty for a Saturday.

At their usual meeting place, Beth knew exactly where Michael would be sitting. By the windows.

As Beth approached him, she saw he'd already purchased their normal orders.

'I thought I was buying this time,' Beth pointed out in greeting as she sat down opposite.

Michael pushed a strand of chocolate brown hair from his face and stared at her with his sea green eyes.

'My treat,' he shrugged. 'You're going through a lot with Emma being gone,'

A silence passed between them for a few moments which was eased a little by the background music. Classical. Orchestra and solo violin. She didn't know the music but recognised it vaguely from an advert, perhaps.

'How much did my order cost?' Beth asked with a raised eyebrow.

'Not much,' was Michael's vague reply as he picked up the receipt and studied it intensely for a few minutes.

Beth watched him as he looked back up at her.

'It was around £5.50,' he replied.

In response Beth reached into her bag and dug around inside until she found her purse and slid over the appropriate change towards him.

'You don't need to pay for it. It's my treat, honestly,' Michael insisted in reply.

Beth was more than aware that she'd always been stubborn, and she couldn't help it. She also knew how much he hated it.

'I'm giving you money for it,' Beth replied, in a warning tone that showed she wasn't going to give up the fight.

'Fine.' It was his turn to give up the fight. He sighed and took the change she'd previously slid across the table towards him.

Beth smiled at him, taking a sip of her hot chocolate and a bite out of her lemon and white chocolate muffin.

'Do you have all of your coursework on you?' she asked.

'Yeah,' he replied, gathering all of the stuff that he needed out of his bag and placing it on the table.

Beth pulled the textbooks out of her own bag and smiled encouragingly at him.

'Let's get started.'

Emma: The Dress

Emma opened her mouth to say something, anything, but nothing came out.

What was wrong with her?

She watched in silence as her captor glanced at the red dress on the hanger – the one she'd decided to, and saw his face quickly morph into anger.

'You're wearing that shitty dress?'

He went over to the wardrobe, snatched the dress from the hanger and ripped it down until it looked like a short and skimpy version of itself.

'I think we need to have a little chat, don't you?'

His eyes blazed in fury as he stared at her.

He moved closer to her and she nodded meekly.

'Good. I'm glad you agree.'

She wasn't sure she was ready for what was to come.

'We're going to give you a new identity tonight.'

He paused for a few moments, seeming deep in thought as he added, 'Your name is going to be... Alexis.'

He smiled at her – a monstrous smile entirely lacking warmth.

'You have five minutes to get yourself prepared, so I'd start now if I were you,' he replied gruffly as he turned his back to her.

Staring at herself in the bathroom mirror she saw tangled and wet black hair falling down to her shoulders. She also saw the blossoming of violet bruises on her cheeks.

The girl in the mirror was alien to her.

She was Alexis.

She was a creation bound to her captor, and
Emma suspected that all traces of her old self would
be stripped away by the time he was done with her.

Trying (and failing) to fix her appearance, she
waited obediently outside of the bathroom door in the
hallway.

He pulled her back into her bedroom.

'Get ready. I'll be waiting for you downstairs,'
he spat at her before leaving.

Letting her towel fall to the floor, she
examined herself for any visible bruises or marks.

For once in her life, she wished she had make-
up on hand to cover them up.

Many were on her face – and others were on
her arms from where the needles had been constantly
piercing her skin.

This was her new reality.

Getting dressed, she winced at the reflection
in her mirror. The fire engine red dress that was now
way too short and didn't make her look or feel any
better. Her hair was too short and dark and just drew
attention to her bruises. But perhaps the full-length
masquerade mask lying on the bed would mean many
were covered.

It wouldn't save her in the future, but it might
save her for now.

Hopefully.

When she had a role to play.

Alexis.

Because she couldn't even imagine the
consequences of her failure.

Beth: Michael

'So, you understand how that works now?' Beth questioned as she and Michael highlighted textbooks.

She could have sworn that she heard him wince as his eyes scanned through all their notes.

'Yep, I think so.'

Beth couldn't tell whether this was the truth. She hoped it was, especially if he wanted decent grades at the end of the course.

'So, I just follow that section and use the structure that's been given to me?' he asked.

'Exactly,' Beth beamed at him.

Maybe he wasn't lying after all. Perhaps he did understand.

'I should probably be heading home now,' Beth said, starting to put all her things away.

'Yeah, me too,' he agreed, reloading his own bag.

'See you later,' Michael added, waving at her.

'Thank you for the help. Really.'

He grinned and left the cafe, leaving Beth alone.

'See you on Monday,' she muttered to herself, as he headed out of the door. She watched as the waitress came over to collect the mugs and small plates, then slung her bag over her shoulder and left the building.

She quickly decided that she wasn't going to take the bus. She would walk home instead. It would give her a chance to go through the different things going through her mind, and perhaps make sense of it all. Ideally, she needed to clear her head of everything.

She had loads of coursework that was due

Monday so was keen to clear her head then get home and get things done.

When she eventually did get back, the house was empty, but at least there was a note left on the kitchen counter.

Mum was out with dad again.

Brilliant.

That mum/dad situation wasn't something else she wanted to add to the long list of complications in her life. Sighing heavily, she trudged upstairs.

Things just didn't feel right with Emma gone.

Emma: The Party

Emma began to descend the stairs, moving towards the sounds of laughter and loud music.

She began to notice things she hadn't really seen before on the walls in the hallway, like family photos from years ago.

It was strange. They all seemed to be smiling but they all appeared forced as if there was some underlying family tension ever-present.

Maybe that was why he had ended up like this.

Reaching the doorway into what was likely the main room, she glanced into a mirror, and Alexis stared back at her.

As she took a few more steps closer to the door, the laughter got louder and louder.

Emma could feel the sweat on the back of her neck and on the palms of her hands. Anxiety ran through her as her heart started to race.

This was the most that she had ever seen of the house. So far, she'd been restricted to the confines of her bedroom, with just occasional glimpses of the bathroom.

Loud music soon became intermingled with the sound of laughter. A slither of light was creeping through the crack in the door.

The light was lucky.

It could escape.

Peeking through the door, she watched as a woman began to flirt with the man she knew only as her captor.

Emma felt sick but also felt something else – envy.

Envy that she couldn't let somebody touch her without flinching, and that she no longer had the freedom she craved.

Taking a deep breath, she made sure that she was standing up straight and the smile that she had fixed onto her face looked completely and utterly genuine. It must have worked because everyone who looked at her when she entered grinned back warmly. She knew there was something else behind their smiles.

Did they know what he was doing to her? She couldn't tell.

Mainly it was the men in the room who fixed her with hungry eyes.

Forcing herself not to shudder, she stepped over to the man's side and all the previous chatter instantly ceased.

The intense stares continued for a little while, then the chatting began again, and all eyes left her.

Apart from one set.

Moving her way around the room, she glanced up at the unstable chandelier. It looked as if it would fall down and smash on the floor at any given moment.

That really would kill the party.

Shelves full of paperbacks adorned the walls, as is common in the living areas of many homes. What was unusual was that the spines were facing inward. How would you know which book was which? Were they for show or did he read them?

The long cream table placed against the back wall was piled with food and a variety of drinks.

Cautiously lifting a hand to take some fruit from one of the platters, she noticed it.

The drink she had that night.

The night all her choices had been taken away from her.

Slipping a grape into her mouth and chewing

slowly, she watched as the men twirled around their partners on the floor. The men's suits were almost identical, but the women wore gowns in an assortment of colours. They were clearly the focus of the evening.

Emma shuddered as they danced. They seemed too carefree and almost like they were high on something. She turned away eventually, her heart beating like a drum as she realised that the mask she was wearing had slipped slightly, exposing the bruises on her face.

'There you are!'

Her captor's voice radiated fake happiness but the steely glare that he was giving her told a different story.

Emma bit her lip and fixed a smile onto her face as he forcibly embraced her.

'You should at least have a drink!' he exclaimed, and she held up her champagne flute to show him it was still full to the brim with liquid.

Emma curled her fingers into her palms, pressing down hard, and knew her palms would sting afterwards.

Her happy facade slipped into place with a click.

Her captor grabbed a drink and stood next to her: 'A toast to my girlfriend and our relationship.'

He lifted his glass and the others did the same. Like clockwork.

He put an arm around her waist and pulled her close to him. In turn she faked looking like she was in love with him.

She pulled her façade around herself even further with her loved-up eyes and forced-relaxed posture.

It was all going so well, until he decided to

rub her shoulders.

Emma instantly flinched and her champagne flute went crashing to the floor, leaving shattered glass everywhere.

'Oops, my mistake. I get clumsy sometimes,' Emma laughed nervously. Luckily everyone else in the room seemed uninterested.

Ignoring the broken glass, she tuned into a nearby conversation.

'Alexis and I have been together for two years, haven't we, sweetheart?'

'Yes,' she replied obediently, trying to stop herself from crying out in pain as he pushed down roughly on one of her shoulders.

'Is something wrong?' one of the guys asked, giving her a sly smile. He seemed to know exactly what was going on.

'She's really cute.'

Suddenly one of the guys who'd been talking began to play with a strand of her hair.

It had been creeping up on her, but it was at that moment when the feeling of light-headedness became obvious.

Everything moved in slow motion as Emma watched one of the women pick up the same drink she herself had drunk on the night she was taken.

'No!' she screamed.

Everything went blank.

The Castle

After promptly getting out of bath and drying herself along with her hair, she cast her eyes to the blood red dress that was still staring at her from where it lay on her bed.

It wasn't a dream. Emma was really going to have to go through with this. Whether she wanted to or not, she didn't have a choice.

Taking a deep breath, she sat in front of the full-length mirror and began to think about how she would style her hair.

Normally a maid would be provided for her to undertake this task, but she had decided against it, simply because she was self-sufficient and didn't need anyone to help her do such small things. Deciding on a hairstyle, she slowly put her hair in an up do, with wisps falling around her face.

Approaching her bed, Emma picked up the blood red dress and stared at it for a few minutes.

Why would he be giving her such things?

He only gave things when he was going to take something away.

Dismissing any thoughts about what he would want from her next, she dressed and slipped the mask over her eyes, concealing her identity. Hopefully she wouldn't be noticed, and the bruises would be concealed.

Emma breathed in with no pain for the first time, waiting for the clock to chime and seal her fate for tonight.

Like a reversed Cinderella.

Emma could hardly balance in the heels she was wearing and having a mask over her eyes didn't help either. She was sure that everyone could still see right through her façade, even if they couldn't see the bruises.

Previous experience told her that there were stairs coming up that would lead her into the great hall. It was crucial that she descended the steps slowly, as she was only able to see the world around her through the small eye slits that had been created within her mask.

When she entered the great hall, Emma took a few minutes to survey the room and how richly it had been decorated and transformed. She had to commend them for that.

Whispers rose up around her as she moved, but she was past caring about what was spoken of her. Emma wouldn't be here if she had any choice.

It looked to her as if there were about one hundred and fifty people in the hall. And the vast quantity of silver platters and trays filled with drinks and food also suggested that.

Emma swerved through the crowds easily, all the while keeping an eye on the white chandelier hanging from the ceiling: a chandelier that was close to breaking, falling and crushing everyone in its proximity.

But where was the king?

Emma decided that even seeing him would be preferable to making small talk with the other ladies.

Reaching out for a flute of champagne on a tray, she glanced at the servant and gave him a smile.

'Thank you,'

It was Michael who held the tray and he threw her a grin.

'It's no problem.'

Emma was stunned into silence, but Michael let out a laugh.

'I'm only looking out for you.'

'You don't have to,' Emma insisted, sipping at her champagne.

'I know I don't. I'm doing it because I care about you,' Michael responded.

Emma opened her mouth and was about to reply when she saw the king strolling in. A true royal, with accompanying arrogant smirk and shoulders back.

Emma turned her panicked eyes onto Michael who smiled.

'I'm not leaving.'

'It isn't the time to be stubborn. You need to leave,' she hissed.

Emma couldn't have more innocent blood spilled.

He opened his mouth to argue, but then stopped.

'Okay, I'll go.'

'Thank you,' Emma whispered, her eyes on Cole. She turned away from Michael and immediately sensed that he had disappeared into the crowd.

Impressive.

Keeping her eyes on Cole, she watched as people bowed and talked to him as they moved out of his path. Cole was heading straight towards her.

What had he found out?

As far as she knew, she hadn't done anything tonight that could anger him.

Unless...

Emma jumped out of her skin as Cole grabbed her arm and pulled her sharply into the corner.

'We need to talk,' he snarled.

'What about?'

How could he know about it?

'The medicine the physician gave you, of course.'

He pushed her against the wall.

'Medicine? I don't know anything about medicine,' she lied, swallowing nervously.

'The medicine that is hiding currently under your bed in your chambers.' He smiled in triumph, and Emma watched as he produced one of the vials from his pocket and clenched it tightly in his hand.

'What is the medicine for?' he asked in a tone that demanded an instant answer instantly. It was a tone she knew well.

'My ribs, sire,' Emma replied bluntly.

'They seem fine to me.'

'Not after you cracked them, sire.'

'How dare you accuse me of such things?'

Cole glared at her, slapping her hard across the face.

'I have the bruises to prove it,' Emma snarled, trying to fight back but he grabbed her throat before she could retaliate.

Cole's hands got even tighter around her neck as he dropped the vial, glass shards scattering.

It was becoming hard to breathe.

'Did you tell the physician how you got them?' His fingers tightened even more around her throat.

Emma could feel the life starting to leave her. Not answering, she cried out as he threw her to the floor. The room began to spin, and her vision dimmed.

The Castle: Protection

Recovering from nearly being choked to death, Emma got to her feet and saw Cole chatting to a group of men in suits. It was then that she realised a woman in the corner wearing a turquoise dress was giving her a knowing look.

Emma took a deep breath in and then out, trying to calm down. Her hands were damp, and she tightened her grip on the champagne flute so much that the skin of her palms became alarmingly white.

Did that woman know something, or had she been through something similar?

If she did know anything about what was happening to Emma right now, she would be in trouble if Cole found out she had tried to connect.

Watching as Cole left the room, Emma tried to lock eyes with the woman in the dark turquoise dress and noticed an opening that she could use in order to escape.

Finally catching the woman's eyes properly and gaining her attention, she gestured her hand towards the corridor. Emma needed to know what the woman knew.

Emma headed towards the corridor and out of the corner of her eye, she saw the woman saying something to her date. Soon the woman approached Emma in the corridor, both women seeming as nervous as each other.

'Beth, my lady.'
The woman introduced herself, swooping into a curtsey.

'Just Emma, please,' and Beth nodded.

Beth spoke first.

'I know what he did to you and still does to you.'

Emma stayed silent as Beth spoke a little more. Suddenly, Beth took Emma's hand and slipped a small blue pill into her palm.

'What is it?' Emma asked.

'Something to help you deal with what he does.'

Emma couldn't speak.

Beth turned to go back inside.

'It happened to me. It gets easier.'

Emma watched as her new friend disappeared back into the party.

Beth: Distractions

Beth suddenly jolted awake all of a sudden, finding herself surrounded by loose bits of paper and notebooks from the previous night's cramming to get her assignment work done. She hadn't needed it doing immediately but she wanted it out of the way.

Her hair was sticking up at the back slightly and at the ends.

She had no idea how she was going to sort this one out. That was, if she could manage to sort it out.

An all-consuming light streamed through the window, taking control of the room in an instant.

It was only six o'clock, and way too early for light to start dominating particular areas of its own accord. Beth was craving the sweet release of sleep. She assumed it was late when she'd finally managed to crash the night before.

Forcing herself to get up, she attempted to rub the exhaustion from her eyes. When that didn't work, she decided on a hot shower. It was something that would force her to become a functional human being - at least for a day.

Beth knew that her tutors would notice that her coursework looked slept on, but it didn't matter. She could just put it in a few plastic sleeves, and it would look perfectly pristine.

It probably wouldn't affect her grades that much. Of course, she'd been up all night studying mainly to keep her mind off other things. She could see it being a pattern for the nights to come.

A smell hit her suddenly, wafting up from downstairs. It smelt like eggs and fresh coffee. Was her mum home already?

Beth slipped her pyjama bottoms on and rummaged around in her wardrobe for an outfit to wear to college for the day. Eventually finding one after a few moments of indecision, she made her way downstairs to see what her mum had prepared for her.

When Beth got downstairs, she made an instant beeline for the kitchen and made a move to claim the kettle. She gave her mum a quick glance, but she was still completely silent and acting as if her daughter wasn't standing right there by the kettle.

When her mum did move out the way, she made herself a quick coffee with milk and sugar, but there was still nothing from her mum.

No snide remark. No enquiry about how she was doing. Nothing.

As Beth stirred her coffee, she thought about the torment that college promised. Almost everyone would be talking about how Emma had disappeared so suddenly.

Pushing the thoughts away, she sipped her coffee and ignored how it burned her throat as it went down.

'Beth?' a voice asked, and her head automatically snapped up, as if the movement had been programmed into her. Her mum was talking to her.

'Yeah?'

'Do you need a lift into college?'

This was mum trying to make conversation, although she knew that college didn't start until ten for her on a Monday.

'I don't start college until ten. I'm going for a run first.'

'You shouldn't be going out for runs with everything that's been going on.'

By everything that's been going on, she meant Emma's disappearance and it wasn't as if her mum cared anyway.

Beth sighed heavily. Appeasement was going to be necessary.

'I'll be careful, okay?'

Her mother tightened up.

'Fine. If anything weird happens you call me or go straight to the police.' Her voice made it clear that Beth shouldn't bother arguing back.

'Fine.'

Getting into her running gear which consisted of a simple black top, a black and hot-pink striped jacket, matching sports leggings and black trainers, Beth made the decision that her college bag sort out could wait till after the run she desperately needed.

'How is college going, anyway?'

That was the first question her mother asked when she came downstairs, and it was a question that caused Beth to stop in her tracks.

Her mum was asking about her personal life? That was new.

She chose to reply to the unusual question, 'Yeah, it's alright.'

'Are you having any breakfast?'

'I'll get something after running,' Beth reassured her.

'That's good,' her mother replied in a neutral tone.

Beth had already failed a few units, but this was before Emma had disappeared. Since then it had just been getting worse. Beth wasn't entirely sure about university now, as she wanted to be around for when Emma came back.

'I'm going to head out now.'

'I'll see you later, then.'

Her mum attempted to smile as Beth left and shut the door behind her.

Emma: The Torture Chair

When Emma finally came to her senses, she was lying on a cold and gleaming tiled floor. She shivered as the cold hit her again and again, but still couldn't gather up the strength to move.

Not only was she in unknown surroundings, but she suddenly noticed that she was completely naked.

Jumping up in horror and suddenly finding the ability to move, she saw that the last scraps of her dress had been ripped and thrown around the room.

As she moved around slowly, she could see that it wasn't only just her dress that had been ripped and strewn.

It was everything she had worn.

A dark shade of pink covered her cheeks all of a sudden as she realised what that meant.

Someone had seen every inch of her.

What happened to her last night?

She tried to swallow but her jaw was preventing the movement. When she tried it was as if there were bruises down its entire length.

Seeing a silhouette of an object in the corner of the pitch-black room, she instantly headed towards it, but it proved not to be a good idea.

In front of her was a seemingly normal chair, but when she got closer, she could see the shackles and chains attached to its arms.

Blood had been dripping down from the chair's arms and she soon discovered that the trail stopped where she was lying. As if her body had been dragged over there. But whose was the blood?

She had to consider every single possibility, even though her body ached, and everything felt heavy when she moved.

Three foldable chairs had been placed around the main 'torture chair'. Draped across one of them was a white chiffon robe which she picked up to cover her own naked body, now feelings of self-consciousness were starting to kick in.

Out of curiosity, she ran her hands down the sides of the chair and then slowly took her place on it and tried to imagine what it would be like for someone to be tortured, mentally and physically.

Why was she thinking about such a thing?

It was completely messed up.

Everything in the room was deathly silent, although she could hear a faint buzzing sound which she was sure was the sound of a heater or boiler.

Perhaps a radiator?

Casting away all her disjointed, nonsensical thoughts, she headed in the direction of the door and pushed it open slightly with a shaking hand. Door swinging open with a creak, there was the usual desolate and dimly lit hallway. Oddly, the lights flickered constantly, in an almost cyclical manner.

It was deathly silent in the hallway, and Emma was almost expecting something to jump out at her and make her scream as always happened in the horror movies - but that didn't happen at all.

She began to make her way down the hallway. Her previous nakedness stood her in good stead. Her lack of shoes meant the sounds of her footsteps could hardly be heard.

At least she wouldn't be seen sneaking around. Continuing down the dimly lit corridor, she reached the end and discovered a well-decorated bathroom filled with elaborate paintings and fancy décor. It was a natural conclusion that whoever had bought this house must have been wealthy.

Kneeling in front of one of the sinks, she let

her robe fall off her shoulders and watched it glide onto the floor.

The first thing she saw in the mirrors were the jagged, red and angry scars on her shoulders. The more she scanned her body, the more bruises and scars she discovered.

Who did this to her and why would they do such a thing?

As she heard footsteps, she grabbed the robe, dressed clumsily and attempted to wash her face, cupping the water in her hands frantically as she splashed her face with the liquid.

A man appeared by the door. He had messy dark hair and steely grey eyes.

'Come on,' was all he said, holding out one of his hands for her to take. Leaning on the side of the sink to help prop her up, she slowly began to wander over to him.

'Are you coming with me?' the man, gazing at her with his grey eyes.

Did he do those things to her?

Surely, she would remember. How could anyone forget those eyes?

Hesitating briefly, she pushed all her doubts aside and took the hand that had been outstretched to her.

Beth: Normality

Beth arrived in college a lot earlier than anticipated. She'd managed to time her run to perfection. Getting back home safely and changing into her college clothes after having a shower, her mind was too blank to follow her thoughts.

Today her outfit was slightly more casual than usual – just a simple scarlet top and bootcut denim jeans. Beth slipped her long sleek black hair into an easy and messy ponytail.

Slinging her bag over her shoulder as she always did, Beth was surprised that she hadn't fallen over yet whilst she was running around getting ready. She hoped that she wouldn't fall over her own feet on the way into college. Her boots were new, and she hadn't broken them in yet.

But at college she realised that not everything had gone to plan. She had left her keys at home.

Damn.

Memories flooded back of when she had first started at her college, how paralysed with nerves she was and how she had got over those nerves by making friends.

But Beth was soon broken out of her thought pattern as she heard all the laughter and chatting that was going on around her. As was often the case, it annoyed her.

Those other students in her class… they hardly ever did any work, and they almost always gave her strange looks. She had no idea why.

But she was wise enough to realise that it seemed to always be the case within small groups. They took the piss out of people if they were lonely or on their own. Easy targets. Sad, really.

The Castle

Emma's eyes studied the electric blue pill resting innocently in her palm.

She wouldn't swallow it yet. It wasn't time. Anyway, the pill was the only evidence that she had of Beth ever existing.

But she was tempted. Maybe if she swallowed it, everything bad would go away.

How did Beth know what he did to her? That was her main question.

Perhaps the pill would work? Whatever it did would be better than reality. Maybe she should just swallow it and see what happened.

But that was for later. At that moment the only thing Emma needed to worry about was leaving the masquerade unnoticed. It wouldn't be easy. Peering both ways down the corridor, it suddenly came to her. That was the right time. If she left now, she wouldn't be seen at all.

Emma could taste her freedom and took a small step forward, when she felt a tap on her shoulder and whirled around to see who it was.

'What?' Emma snapped, glaring at the person who had interrupted her escape.

'I'm sorry, my lady,' the servant stammered, flushed in the face. 'I didn't mean to startle you.'

Emma didn't recognise him but was on her guard all the same. He was probably one of Cole's servants. She gave a heavy sigh. Even if he did work for Cole, it wasn't the servant who made her angry.

'I'm sorry for snapping, I'm just jumpy today,' Emma lied with ease, and he seemed to accept her explanation.

'King Cole wishes that you dance with him and has enquired about your whereabouts.'

'Of course.'

Emma's voice was quiet, and close to a whisper. There would be no chance of escape.

As the servant left, she watched the fragile pieces of her escape shatter just as quickly as they had been formed.

Alexis: Beginnings

The girl looked down at their intertwined hands and gave a shy smile, feeling unexpectedly comfortable as the men led her from the bathroom into another room.

She could have sworn that she had seen these surroundings before. It looked as if a party had been held at some point over the last few days. There were expensive-looking plates just thrown on the floor, and bits of food and drink were buried in the carpet. Shards of glass intermixed with all of the mess.

She stumbled and reached down, then winced as one of the glass shards cut her finger. She saw the blood weeping out and realised that the liquid pooling underneath the glass shards had a smell she knew. Was it berries? Where had she smelt that before?

'Here, let me look at that.'

The man took her hand in his and examined the cut on her finger. She let out a sharp wince at the pain.

'Stay there. I'll go and get you a plaster.'

He winked at her and gave her a soft smile.

The girl blushed in response.

'Thank you,' she murmured. He nodded, disappeared and soon returned with a plaster that he wrapped securely around her cut.

'All better,' he said, reaching down and kissing the finger. That made her blush even more.

He sat in a chair. She remained standing.

'What's my name?' she asked. It was a question that had been floating around her head for a while.

She couldn't just be without a name.

'I don't remember much,' she added, watching him pause with a slow smile and only the most minor hesitation.

'Your name is Alexis.'

It sounded suitable.

'How do I know you?' Alexis asked, moving strands of her short raven black hair out of her face.

'We're good friends,' he said quietly, looking at her bruised body. 'I'm sorry about what happened to you last night, I tried to stop them.' He trailed off, looking down at his hands.

Alexis frowned, 'What happened to me?

He just shook his head. 'I need to carry on cleaning up this room.'

Alexis nodded in response, but she needed to find out he had started pulling away when she asked him about their relationship.

They both worked together to clear up the mess, and it gradually disappeared as if it had never been there in the first place.

He then took a seat next to her.

'Are you okay?'

'Yeah,' Alexis replied and forced a smile. Blurred recollections of the previous night's events were still circling around in her mind.

'I think we should introduce ourselves again,' he murmured. 'Make a new start.'

'I agree,' Alexis replied, smiling for real this time.

'I'm Cole.'

He held out a hand for her to shake.

'Alexis,' she grinned and shook his hand firmly.

Beth: Class

Beth reached into her bag and pulled out everything that she needed for her first class. One of the things was her old-style iPod that she had borrowed from one of her family members years ago, along with the charger lead that she used frequently within lessons to charge her phone up.

Tapping her fingers against the desk, she realised that the tutor was half an hour late, so she might as well begin to continue with her other assignments while she was waiting.

Apparently, nothing had changed.

Sometimes the tutors didn't even show up.

While she was working on her assignment on the computer in front of her, she opened her news app on her charging phone. If anything came through about Emma, she wanted to be the first to know. And, not being immediate family, she wouldn't get any information from the police.

She couldn't even go and ask them as she'd never met any of Emma's family, Emma being quite a private person. But she'd picked up something about the mother. That small child had expected her mother to be around her to love and nurture her as she grew up. That was the role of the mother, right? Probably not in Emma's case.

Beth was now halfway through her assignment and hadn't even realised how well she'd been working. Writing the assignment came easy to her when she was in the mood for it, but, unlike Emma, Beth found the phrasing and other parts of work challenging.

Shaking her head, Beth put her earphones in, turned up music on her phone and carried on.

The Castle

Still standing in the hallway, Emma couldn't believe that her plans of escape had been ripped to pieces in a single moment.

But she could understand how he could predict what she was going to do. After all, he had held her against her will for a very long time. Emma didn't even know herself anymore.

Emma made sure that her dress had been dusted down but noticed that it had been damaged in places. Ignoring the sinking feeling in her chest, she forced herself to stand up straight like a queen would. She forced herself to find a reason to stay strong.

As she headed back into the ballroom, she realised that the party was in full swing and didn't look as if it would be stopping anytime soon. Most of the people in the ballroom had been separated into colours, couples matching each other.

Glancing down at her torn scarlet dress, she forced herself to make her way to Cole who was standing on the opposite side of the ballroom. He held out his hand and she reluctantly accepted.

After all, she had a part to play tonight and she was only doing what she was told.

Beth: Evidence

Beth's classes had soon finished for the day and she'd also finished a few assignments for one of the modules - but couldn't anticipate the grade she might achieve.

She overheard two people talking and she realised that they were repeating the same mixed rumours going around about someone new joining her class. Apparently, the person was coming from another college as he hadn't got all the grades.

While she was walking home, she noticed two friends who were laughing and joking together, and obviously having fun. Beth hadn't realised that she'd stopped, frozen, in the middle of the pavement and was staring at them.

Just like Emma and Beth had been.

Realising that she'd been staring, she made her way in the direction of her home. It wouldn't take long for her to get back.

Walking into the house, Beth shivered at how quiet and tense the atmosphere was.

'Mum?' she called out, heading into the living room where she saw her mum sitting on the living room sofa staring ahead. She glanced at her mum nervously, as she was as white as a sheet.

'What's wrong?' she asked.

Her mother took a deep breath.

'The police found evidence that Emma was kidnapped.'

Beth had to grab the side of the kitchen counter to steady herself, and she was shocked to realise that a slight sense of happiness ran through her. Beth wasn't happy because there was evidence that her best friend had been kidnapped - that would just be horrible. She was happy because one of her theories had been right. Emma hadn't run away like everyone had suspected.

Beth stayed quiet for a while.

'So, we don't know who took her?' she asked in a shaky voice.

'Not yet.'

Her mum moved around Beth to flick the kettle on and made a coffee for herself. She couldn't look at Beth.

'Do we even know if she's alive?'

Beth was eager to drink up any information that she could obtain about Emma's kidnapping/disappearance.

There was no response.

If Beth's hunches about Emma not running away were right, might her hunches about Emma not being dead also be correct?

'The police are coming in a few hours.'

'Why?'

'To ask you some questions.'

Her mum bit her lip, her tone suggesting that she disagreed with the whole idea.

Beth ran a hand through her hair in frustration. Questions like what?

Would they try to frame her for something?

That was when the panic set in, and it was panic than ran deep inside of her.

'I'm going upstairs,' Beth announced, panic clouding her judgement completely as she practically ran upstairs. Escape to her room seemed the only option. She slammed the door shut.

How much did the police know?

What kind of leads did they have?

Did they think she killed her?

Beth flipped open her laptop and bit her lip as

her eyes scanned through all the news articles. She also read and re-read a document she'd created which she'd populated with loads of notes on Emma's case.

Beth's best friend was out there as the hostage of some complete and utter maniac that wanted her for his own twisted reasons.

Beth didn't want to think about the perverted things that guy might be thinking.

If she didn't try to help, who would?

Besides, who knew Emma better than Beth did?

Beth heard a knock at the door and her anxiety skyrocketed. She decided to stay completely silent.

Alexis: Waking Up

Surveying the living room from top to bottom and noticing all the vintage furniture, Alexis realised how attractive the room was. She would be more than happy staying there.

As Cole disappeared into the kitchen, Alexis considered what had happened only a few hours ago. What he had told her made sense so far. There was no reason at all to doubt him.

'Do you want a drink?' His voice came out muffled as he was in the room adjacent to hers.

'Yes please!' she called back in enthusiastic response. She was quite happy with anything that she got right now, as long as the drink was something that could rid her of her dry throat.

Cole soon came out of the kitchen holding two glasses filled to the brim with liquid and she took it from him gladly. Raising it to her mouth and taking a sip, she sighed in relief.

She set her glass down onto the side table next to her as Cole collapsed onto the sofa.

'Is there anything you want to know that I haven't explained to you already?' Cole asked.

'Why can't I remember anything?' Alexis asked as the question had been ready and waiting inside her mind.

'The accident wiped your memory.'

He frowned, and suddenly seemed sad.

Had she said something wrong?

Cole must have seen the expression on her face because he touched her shoulder lightly.

'It's not you. It's just the fact I nearly lost you.' He cast his eyes to the ground.

'What happened to me?' Alexis pressed, eager and desperate to know the truth.

'Someone broke in and attacked you before I could do anything to stop them.'

Cole couldn't meet her eyes.

So that was why she had all the bruises and cuts on her body. It explained the blood in that room too.

'Are the bruises bad?' he asked softly.

Alexis nodded and moved away from him slightly, hesitant to show him the bruises.

'Let me see,' he replied gently and bit his lip when Alexis let her robe shrug off her shoulders slightly.

She watched as Cole frowned and reached out to touch the bruises on her thigh.

'You wouldn't remember it,' he said quietly. 'It's shocking that you don't remember anything from your past either. My parents died when I was younger, much like yours did,' he murmured, frowning as if in recollection of painful memories.

'My parents died?' Alexis replied, in shock.

She received only a nod in response.

'My father abused my mother for years and it eventually drove her to suicide. That's why I killed him.' He moved his hand away from her thigh. His voice sounded like he was in a distant place, hollow and empty.

'You did what you had to,' Alexis replied in a reassuring tone and made sure that her voice didn't go higher than a whisper.

Cole went quiet before his face became completely blank and void of all emotion.

'Would you mind finishing the washing up from the party? I need to be alone right now.'

'Of course.' Alexis gave him a gentle smile and went into the kitchen.

The Castle

'So, why did you run?'

Cole's voice brought her back to the present. Suddenly she remembered where she was, and the dancing couples around them told her everything that she needed to know.

She stayed as quiet as a mouse, but the sharp tug on her arm demanded an answer.

'I needed a new life,' was all Emma replied, her voice a vacant monotone. She wasn't going to give him the satisfaction of provoking a reaction out of her.

He stared at her for a few minutes, then burst out laughing manically.

'Were you under the impression that I would let you escape, regardless of how much you wanted freedom?' A look of mock curiosity crossed his face.

Emma tried to busy herself to provide a reason for her silence, but Cole continued.

'At least you aren't dead,' he pointed out. He paused dramatically. 'Yet.' His smile was triumphant.

'I can fight my way out of any situation,' she said to herself. No way was she a damsel in distress and she would always make her own destiny, dealing with everything that came her way, including abusive and arrogant kings. It was a few seconds later that she figured out she'd spoken those thoughts out loud.

'I'm sure.'

He inclined his head in a slight mock bow and let go of her waist so suddenly that she stumbled and fell straight onto the floor.

Beth: The Police

Venturing downstairs to the bathroom, Beth didn't expect to be pulled into the interview with her mother.

'Does anyone want tea or coffee?' she asked, glancing at the police officers sitting on either side of her mum.

'Sure,' one of them replied and her mother nodded too. Beth tried to remember the milk and sugar requests as she went into the kitchen and put the kettle on.

She could hear the chatter from the living room and all the questions that were being asked. She even paused for a few minutes to listen.

Beth finished making the drinks and took them into the living room in rounds.

One of the police offers stood up, 'Beth, is it? Can we talk to you for a few minutes?'

Beth nodded but stayed quiet, sitting down and resting her eyes on the steaming mug of tea in front of her.

She wasn't the only person in the world to feel uneasy at having police round, even though she'd done nothing wrong.

Alexis: Housework

Alexis's arms ached from the quantity of the washing up, and because she wanted to complete it to a high standard so Cole would be proud of her. She allowed him to view her handiwork, and he seemed pleased.

'That's well done,' Cole praised, grinning from ear to ear at her, obviously proud of all her efforts.

'Thanks.'

She gave a small smile in return.

'You should probably go and have a lie down, as you were up most of last night.'

Alexis couldn't really remember anything, but it must have been true as she was feeling quite tired.

'I'll bring you up something to eat and drink.'

'Okay,' Alexis murmured in response, letting a yawn slip out of her lips.

She was about to go upstairs when she hesitated slightly. 'Where is my room?' she asked.

'I'll show you.'

Cole followed her upstairs, leading her down the corridor and towards the door at its end.

He opened the door.

'Alright?' he asked.

Alexis nodded and headed inside.

Of course, she didn't see that Cole had locked the door.

The Castle

Emma rose up from her fall onto the dusty ballroom floor, fighting back tears as she heard the whispers and laughter of the other lords and ladies echoing throughout her ears and mind.

Everyone laughed. All apart from Beth. Her new friend was looking at her with sympathy written plainly on her face.

Beth had offered her a way out and given her some kind of hope. She hadn't felt anything similar to that in a long time.

When Emma slipped her hand into the pockets of her dress, she was calmed when she found that the pill was still safe in a secret corner. She left the room quickly and the humiliation she had felt just a few minutes ago melted away like wax on a candle.

She would return to her chambers. She needed to distance herself from everyone and everything. Most of the court people were fake, but Beth wasn't. She was genuine. She was real.

She was her only real friend and maybe everything would work out this time.

Emma hoped so. She hadn't had a real friend in a long time.

Beth: Meeting Joe

Waking up, Beth was irritated both by the fact her alarm hadn't gone off yet, and also by the remnants of her violent and vivid nightmare.

She took herself over the day. First would be college, and later there would be tutoring with Michael again. It was the only time that she could do it this week, so she couldn't cancel.

Her alarm's malfunction, and the physical remains of her nightmare provided a less than brilliant start to her day, especially when she was completely exhausted.

Glancing out of her window, Beth realised for the first time that the rain was falling gently onto the ground. Embracing her mood and the weather around her, she looked in the depths of her wardrobe for something appropriate to wear.

She pulled out a grey Radiohead shirt and a pair of obsidian leggings and matched them with her favourite ankle boots. Tying her hair into a messy ponytail, she went downstairs and was met with complete silence.

She went into the living room, and there was her mum still wrapped up in pyjamas, curled up on the sofa watching the news on mute and staring blankly at the screen.

'Mum? Are you okay?' Beth asked as she approached her mother slowly.

'I'm fine.'

Her Mum was obviously lying as there was absolutely nothing behind her eyes or behind her voice at all.

'Beth?' her mum said suddenly.

Beth swivelled around instantly.

'Yeah?' Beth asked.

'Emma's dad gave me a ring. He needs help putting flyers and posters up.' She sounded sad. Perhaps her mum had been more affected by Emma's disappearance than Beth had originally thought.

Emma's dad had never even met Beth, but it seemed like Emma must have told him about their friendship.

'Tell him I'll get there as soon as I can,' Beth said.

'Please be careful when you're out, even if it is just at college.'

'I will be careful, mum, I always am.'

After slipping her shoes on and making sure that she had everything that she needed, she left the house quickly and shut the door behind her.

It had been a while since she had been to Emma's house to hang out or sleepover, but even then, she had never encountered any of Emma's family. They had been arguing quite a lot within the first four months of their friendship, but she couldn't remember what it was about.

Beth may have been almost alone here, but she didn't want to go back to her old college and become her old self again. She had been a bitch back then.

Trying to prevent the memories from coming back, she headed into her classroom and handed all her work to her tutor, before sitting down at her normal seat. It was only then that she discovered somebody new was sitting next to her.

Weird.

Hardly anyone ever sat next to her.

But it wasn't a massive issue. She was only waiting for her work to be marked before she could go home.

'Is that a Radiohead shirt?' a voice piped, causing her to look up.

'Yeah,' Beth smiled warmly.

'Pretty cool,' he replied. 'I like 'OK Computer' the best.

'Same here!' Beth exclaimed, watching as the newcomer opened all the assignment sheets their tutor had indicated.

'I'm new to the course. Is there any chance that you could help me with the assignment work?'

'Sure.'

'I'm Joe,' the guy said.

'Beth,' she replied and moved over to help him. It was only until her work had been marked, but then she had to leave and help Michael.

The Castle

Arriving outside of the door that allowed her to enter her chambers, she provided herself with a strict mental note that she hoped she could always remember.

The pill was in her pocket, ready for if she needed it. Entering the chambers, Emma winced as she was blinded by the light streaming from between her blinds.

Emma couldn't remember opening them but considering how the day had been unfolding she wasn't surprised.

It wasn't long before her eyes adjusted to the light and she realised that there was a note on her pillow. First making sure there was nobody else in the corridors, she opened the note and read it.

Beth wanted to meet her tomorrow. She wanted to talk. Emma would go the next day. Not wanting to leave any evidence behind, she threw the note into the roaring fireplace.

Beth: Meeting Emma's Dad

After finishing up with Michael in their usual coffee shop, Beth pondered on what her Mum had said earlier - that Emma's dad needed to talk to her. Emma's house wasn't that far from the town centre so Beth was pretty sure she could make it there on foot. It would only take about fifteen minutes.

As she walked, she remembered all the times she'd met up with Emma in town and they had walked this way together.

Something that crossed her mind all of a sudden was wondering how Emma's dad had got her number in the first place. The only way that he'd know about her, was if Emma talked about her often.

The walk to Emma's house was lost in thoughts but fear gripped Beth as she took the final few steps to Emma's door.

Gingerly, she raised her hand to the door and knocked a few times with trembling fingers. Beth could see a shadowy figure coming towards the door which soon swung open in front of her.

Emma's dad stood silently and stared down at Beth, his light blue eyes holding a vacant expression, his brown hair messy and as if he hadn't washed it in days. He had a defeated aura about him, like he had given up on everyone and everything.

Beth wasn't surprised about how sickly and exhausted he seemed to be, especially after everything the family was going through.

'Come in, come in.'

She was ushered into the living room and scanned it quickly. She noticed that nothing had changed since she'd been there last - apart from the alcohol bottles that were piling up in the bins.

Was nobody helping him through this?

'Do you want anything to drink?' he asked as she sat down on the sofa.

'A coke, please, if you have one,' Beth replied.

He nodded. 'I have some. For Emma. I'll be one minute.' He got up and went into the kitchen.

Beth heard him as he opened the fridge, unscrewed the bottle and poured the liquid.

She knew that he was like her. Not functioning properly. Hanging off the edge of a cliff while he searched meaninglessly for answers.

Out of curiosity, she went over to the corner of the room and found tons of open cardboard boxes.

Boxes of flyers and posters.

This time she didn't stop the tears running down her face.

Alexis: Fatigue

Alexis opened her eyes. She must have fallen asleep at some point, but she couldn't remember when or how. All she did know for certain was that she still felt absolutely exhausted.

Snippets of nightmares flew around her head that prevented her from waking up completely, but the smell of tea started to bring her out of her dazed state.

Where was it coming from?

Jolting out of bed and thinking that she had just imagined the smell, she discovered that a mug of tea had been placed innocently on her bedside table.

She remembered Cole from the previous day but was still searching for any recognition or recollection from before then. But she emerged with absolutely nothing. Every time she tried, she hit a mental brick wall.

After downing her tea, she made the decision that she should probably get out of bed and get dressed. She had no idea if Cole had a schedule for the day and how everything worked in his home. Their home?

Making her way over to the wardrobe, she pulled out the first two items of clothing that were hanging up in the wardrobe and carefully placed them on the bed. A mustard yellow crop top and shiny black leggings.

A few minutes after getting dressed, she heard a noise behind her and spun around to see Cole standing in the doorway.

Was he even allowed in her room without knocking? Were there no ground rules between them?

Alexis hesitated before looking back up at Cole.

'Morning,' she said.

'Did you enjoy your tea?' he asked, a smile appearing on his face which didn't quite meet his eyes.

'It was really nice, thanks.'

She wiped her lips quickly, hoping there were no remains of the drink dripping down her lips.

'I have a present for you downstairs.'

He turned away from her and left suddenly.

Beth: Potential Suspects

Emma's dad emerged from the kitchen with two glasses both filled to the brim with fizzy liquid. Beth assumed, and hoped, that it was coke.

His eyes fell as she stared at the posters and flyers.

'You found the flyers,' he said, and they stared at the pictures of Emma and Beth together, both girls smiling as if they didn't have a care in the world.

'Yeah.'

Beth trailed off, unsure of what to say next

'Are you updated with police information?' Emma's dad asked, breaking the awkward silence. His eyes were tired and red.

'All I know is that they have evidence proving that she was kidnapped.'

'So, you didn't know about the potential suspects?'

It was a question that immediately grabbed Emma's attention.

The Castle

Emma heard a sudden noise from behind her and a shock ran through her body.

Why was he here?

She just wanted to prevent it somehow. She knew what was coming, and all she could taste in her mouth was dirt.

She didn't have to turn to know it was Cole behind her. She could see him in her mirror. She could see how he stared at her with his intense pitch-black eyes.

Finding a glass of crystal-clear liquid by her bedside, she remembered the baby-blue pill hidden away in her pocket. All she needed to do was swallow it without him seeing.

Edging closer to her bedside table, Cole swore under his breath and left the room.

Emma couldn't think about that now. She needed to take the pill while she still had the chance. Snatching the glass from the bedside table and the pill from her pocket, she swallowed it down.

She knew what was going to happen as he appeared again behind her, this time with a smirk engraved onto his face.

'Please,' Emma begged, knowing that her begging was to no avail.

Why wasn't the pill working?

That was when she heard a quiet click and Emma was suddenly standing near her own body. She wasn't within it. She was outside of it.

It took a few minutes to realise that she wasn't standing but floating...

Shaking her head, she quickly turned away from Cole and what seemed to be her body, while they...

No.

Emma wasn't going to stay here to see this. It was surprising though. She wasn't feeling any pain at all.

Getting up and walking out of the door, she did notice one small detail - a chain linking this form to her body.

Emma didn't understand, but she had been given a chance to escape and it would be stupid not to take the chance.

Alexis: The Present

Why would he give her a present?

She followed the echo of his footsteps downstairs and stood next to him in the hallway.

'Can I get a clue?' Alexis asked eagerly.

'No,' he replied, smirking.

'Fine.'

That was when Alexis felt something cover her eyes - and she was left in darkness. The texture felt like silk. Cole was behind her pushing and guiding her through what she could only assume were multiple rooms. Then the blind fell off to reveal a present wrapped in ocean-blue paper and lying on the floor.

'One second,' Cole murmured, producing something out of his pocket.

A camera?

Why would he need a camera?

'I want to record this so we can look back on it,' he explained.

'Oh, right. Okay. It's a good idea,' she said with an enthusiastic tone to her voice.

She wasn't concerned about the camera. All she wanted to do was rip open the present in front of her.

It was an easel and multipacks of canvases.

'Thank you!' she exclaimed, hugging Cole tightly as he stroked her hair and laughed.

'No problem.'

He shut the camera off and put it to one side.

'I have paint you can use. Shall we go set it up?'

Alexis nodded and followed him, fuelled with happiness like a small child on Christmas morning.

Beth: The Boxes

'What do you mean, potential suspects?'

The police hadn't mentioned anything about that. But why would they mention anything to her?

'They're looking at her two blonde friends and some guys that they knew,' he replied, shrugging. 'I didn't recognise them.'

'Can you remember their names?' Beth asked.

'I think they were...' He trailed off, obviously under strain from trying to remember, before sighing and giving up.

'I can't.'

'That's okay,' Beth replied reassuringly. There was no way she wanted to push the limits too much. If he couldn't remember anything, then she had to take his word for it.

'You should go and put those posters up now,' Emma's dad prompted. Beth knew that this was a signal for her to leave and get on with the job that she was supposed to be doing.

She carried out a couple of the small boxes in a carrier bag but didn't realise that her bag had been left on the floor.

Beth: Ghosts

Beth woke up after a while, her arms and legs aching from all the work she had done the day before.

'Are you off college today?' her mum asked while they both ate breakfast, everything seemingly back to their normal routine. Her mum seemed a lot calmer.

'Nope, I still should go in, even though I'm just waiting to get everything marked,' Beth replied, groaning slightly.

'You better get going then.' Her mum checked the time on her phone as her daughter did.

'Yeah, I probably should.'

'How long are you in for?'

'I'm not sure. Maybe all day, but I might get out earlier... I'll text you.'

'Okay.'

Beth felt her mother's eyes on her as she walked out of the door and headed head off to college.

The Castle

It was the next morning that Emma found herself tangled up in her very own bedsheets, sunlight hitting her naked form. The last thing she remembered was being outside of her body entirely.

Shaking her head, she glanced down slowly at the bed, and blood-stained mattress, and she felt herself shudder involuntarily, the pain and soreness creeping in suddenly. At least she knew that the pill had worked for her. The only side effects seemed to be all that had happened to her body that only came back to her when she was re-attached.

Deciding that she was going to have a bath to wash everything away, including the pain and the feelings that ran with it. She would push everything that had happened right to the back of her mind.

Emma watched the water as it gushed out of the taps and slowly filled up the bath.

That was when she remembered something. The thought erased replaced the strange invasive feelings crawling over her body with something a lot cleaner.

She was meeting Beth later. Perhaps Beth could provide her with the answers she needed. It wouldn't be too hard to track down her down - at least that's what she hoped.

If Cole found out about them meeting, they would both be in trouble, but she would probably be in more trouble than Beth.

She gave a sudden shudder at that thought, but she would have to come up with a way to get out of the situation when she happened to stumble into it.

~

After getting out of the bath and changing into comfortable clothing, she left her chambers and ventured into the corridor.

Memories crept back into her mind like a depression. This was how she had escaped the kingdom last time and the corridors were empty now, exactly the way they had been last time.

She could just escape again now, but it seemed too easy. She was surprised that the whole castle wasn't under heavy guard. She fought her urge to run in the other direction. Instead she composed herself, controlled her emotions and headed for the gardens.

Emma wasn't running away this time.

Beth: Lost Bag

Beth paused suddenly as she reached the bus stop.

Shit.

She left her bag over at Emma's house with her purse and other important items inside of it. For some reason, it hadn't even occurred to her yesterday, but she should have remembered.

Could she manage going back to that house? Well, she was going to have to. Even if she didn't have time to go back.

Glancing at her phone again nervously, she decided that she would have enough time and wouldn't be staying there long anyway. Feeling the absence of her possessions, she carried on walking in the direction of Emma's house.

Alexis: The Painting

When her first painting was finally complete, Cole helped Alexis frame it and she stared at it for a while.

It was strange to see her art actually framed and presented on a wall. From what she could gather, not many artists received appreciation for what they did.

'What do you think?' Alexis asked nervously as Cole viewed the painting, seemingly deep in thought about the content.

'It's good, although I see what you mean about the nose.' He grabbed a packet of cigarettes from a side table and lit one, taking a long drag.

Alexis simply shrugged, not really knowing what to say in response. She had already decided that she was going to busy herself with cleaning to keep her mind off of his opinion of her work.

It was crucial to her that he liked it. His opinion mattered to her.

Alexis began the cleaning and jumped at the sound of Cole's voice.

'Need any help with that?' he asked.

'Yeah sure,' she mumbled, yanking her hand back as they eventually touched from going to pick up the brushes at the same time.

Beth: The Note

After a few hours she had made it safely over to Emma's house for the second time.

Before she could open the door, it had been opened for her.

Emma's dad stood in the doorway as he had the first time.

'You're here to pick up your bag,' he said, producing the bag from behind his back.

'Yeah, how did you...' Beth trailed off in surprise.

He pushed her bag towards her.

'You might find something in there that will help you find my daughter.'

He glanced at the bag as if he was scared it was going to disappear any second.

'You knew her better than I do,' he added.

Beth didn't say much but took her bag from him.

'I suggest you leave.'

A cold tone took over his voice. He shut the door and left Beth completely stunned.

She rummaged her hands through the bag that she had lost, making sure that everything was there, which it was.

But it was then that she found something interesting. It was something that she knew had never been in her bag.

She pulled the item out. It was a phone with a note attached to it. The note read:

You can do a better job than the police can.

It was Emma's cracked phone that she was holding.

Alexis: Evidence

When Alexis woke up, it was obvious that the atmosphere had completely changed.

From what she could hear coming from elsewhere in the house, something had fallen to the floor. Her blood suddenly ran cold.

Had someone broken into the house?

Assuming that Cole was still asleep, she pulled the robe from the back of her door, slipped it on and tied it around her waist to keep herself warm.

Pushing the door open, she realised that she hadn't locked it the previous night. How stupid, specially when someone could have broken in.

Against the advice that her racing heart was giving her, she carried on moving downstairs until she was at the bottom. Alexis could see lights flickering on and off, and knew the lights were in the kitchen. She would need to talk to Cole about fixing his lights.

She slipped through the living room and stopped by the entrance to the kitchen. Her robe swept across the floor silently in her wake.

One of the first thing she noticed when she walked into the kitchen was all the broken glass. The second was a cupboard that was slightly ajar.

A figure emerged from the shadows, and the figure cried out in pain as he knelt down on the floor. A sigh of relief escaped her lips as she realised that it was only Cole.

'You should still be in bed.'

Cole frowned at her in disapproval, his voice was quieter than usual.

'Sorry.' Alexis looked down, feeling like a child who had been scolded by a strict parent.

'I was only worried about you,' she added, concern creeping into her voice as she saw the blood pulsating from his wound and dripping down his finger.

Beth: Crucial Evidence?

If this was Emma's phone residing in her bag, she had a piece of crucial evidence connected to Emma's kidnapping. There could be serious repercussions for her if the police knew she had it. She might even end up becoming a suspect in Emma's disappearance.

Pushing everything that wasn't college-related out of her brain, Beth forced her body to venture inside the building, even though she knew there was no point in even coming into college anymore. She would grin and bear it until her work was marked and everything was sorted.

Eventually conjuring up the willpower to enter her classroom, she sat in her normal seat near the back row of the classroom and turned to see the guy from yesterday sitting once again in the seat next to hers.

'Hey.' He greeted her as she sat down.

'Hey,' Beth replied, grinning to herself. She was still glowing from the fact that she actually made a friend who seemed like an alright person.

They chatted through the next two lessons about their hobbies and interests. Intriguingly they had many similar interests, and both loved reading and playing games, though he was a lot more experienced in gaming.

After they had swapped numbers, Beth realised that it was lunchtime.

'I might just bail and go home. I mean, I don't have any work to do,' Beth shrugged.

'Okay,' he replied, 'I'll see you soon, then?' He was still hunched over his work on the computer screen as he caught up on all his assignments.

'Can I take you out tomorrow night?'

Beth stopped and stood completely still.

'Sure,' was her quick response, given as she walked away so he couldn't see her blush.

When she got home, the first thing she did was to dig the phone out of her bag again, staring at it for a few minutes, eyes wide as if she had seen a ghost.

Beth had to do this.

She clicked the home button and watched Emma's phone come to life. From the look of it, the phone was still fully charged. Perhaps Beth should've asked whether it had been touched before it had been passed over to her for inspection.

The Castle

Emma took the corridor that led her into the garden and was shocked when she realised that all of the plants and flowers seemed to be wilting slightly - dying even.

This was a strange thing. The garden always looked beautiful, and in full bloom. But now all the plants seemed lifeless, as if nobody had been taking care of them for a very long while.

Many of the children used to play within the garden during summer months. It was the only pure and innocent thing that hadn't been corrupted in this place.

With a heavy heart that kept sinking rapidly, Emma studied the gardens and trudged through the weeds left in the shadow of the dying blooms.

Emma was probably ruining her gown, but that didn't matter to her right now.

The only thing that mattered was trying to find Beth. Maybe she had forgotten all about the meeting that she arranged. Emma wouldn't be surprised, as she herself was extremely forgetful at times.

Emma didn't know Beth or her motives. Sighing heavily, Emma scanned around to try and find anything that might assist her. That was it. A tree. She sat beneath it for shelter and comfort.

Time was trickling away like water in a sink, and she could only wait. Maybe it was just a set-up and she should just leave before she embarrassed herself any further than she already had.

After a few hours, Beth was still nowhere to

be seen.

Emma stood up and brushed herself down slowly, but Emma didn't care anymore if her gown was tattered.

All she needed was the strength and ability to lie that would save her from Cole. She knew that anyone that close to her would most likely die at Cole's hand. Even knowing her was dangerous if she slipped up.

She had almost given up when she saw that Beth was walking towards her. So, Beth was going to be loyal to Emma after all. Maybe she shouldn't have doubted her in the first place. Beth was looking around in confusion, so Emma signalled for Beth to come over to her.

'Emma,' Beth greeted. She was wearing a royal blue cloak with the hood up to obscure her face.

'Beth,' Emma replied, flicking her hair out of her eyes as the wind began to pick up.

'What did you want to talk about?'

Emma glanced at her, sudden rain pouring down from the skies, causing Beth to take cover under the same tree that Emma had chosen.

'Let's get inside and then we can talk about it,' Beth murmured. Emma simply nodded.

Alexis: Trauma

Alexis stood frozen to the spot. She couldn't tear her eyes away from the blood or make an advance towards Cole to help him.

Drip.

Drip.

Drip.

That was the sound that the blood made as it fell onto the floor, like a tap that hadn't been tightened properly and had instead been left to fill up a sink with its excess water.

Why did she feel as if she had seen something like that before?

'How did you do it?' Alexis asked him, managing to break out of her previous trance.

'What?' Cole looked taken aback for a second.

'The cut on your hand.'

'Oh, that? That's nothing.'

Alexis could see him biting his lip because of the pain but said nothing at all about it.

'Doesn't look like nothing.'

Cole gave a heavy sigh, 'I said it was nothing, alright?' His snapping causing Alexis to fall silent.

She flinched and jumped back into the shadows, most of her body hidden in an attempt to keep herself safe.

As if sensing her fear, Cole frowned and knelt closer to her.

'I'm sorry, I shouldn't have snapped at you like that.'

Something about Cole made Alexis feel as if there was no sincerity behind his words, but that may have just been her paranoia talking. He had been nothing but nice to her.

'It's alright, I'm sorry I annoyed you.'

Alexis's voice was quiet and soft, but not quite a whisper.

'It's okay. Friends?' Cole asked her, holding his arms out for an embrace.

'Friends,' Alexis confirmed and accepted the hug happily. His hugs made her feel warm and protected.

'Now, go upstairs and act surprised to see that your breakfast has been made.'

He nudged her and she pulled away from him contentedly.

'Okay,' Alexis giggled, and Cole's deep and throaty laugh soon mixed in with hers.

It was the first time that Alexis remembered hearing Cole laugh and it was an amazing sound.

What Alexis hadn't seen was the smirk that had been plastered over Cole's face when he let go of her.

Sleep became easy for Alexis when she climbed back into bed.

The Castle

Emma followed Beth quickly, trying to keep up with her pace.

'Where are we going?' Emma asked.

'A place that I found a few years ago,' Beth explained.

When Beth eventually came to a stop, Emma found herself looking up at a huge treehouse. She had never seen it before on all her walks around the gardens.

Heading in after Beth, Emma took in her surroundings and realised that it looked like someone had been living inside the treehouse on and off.

Drink cans and food wrappers had been scattered around on the floor. It was then that Emma noticed the chocolate-brown moth-eaten sofa in the corner. It only confirmed her suspicions.

'How long have you been living here?' Emma asked.

Beth paused, 'Sometimes a few days or a few months. It depends.'

She shrugged.

There was a sudden silence between them, and Beth ended up patting the empty seat next to her on the sofa as she sat down.

Emma sat down next to Beth. She couldn't help but be intrigued. She wanted to talk to Beth some more, and to try and figure out how she had become the person that she was today.

'I was his ward once. I thought I was protected,' Beth started, her eyes fixed on shadows cast on the opposite wall. 'But you know what happened there.' Beth's voice was suddenly lowered, and she fixed Emma with a dark gaze.

Suddenly Emma understood. They were both survivors and they were both living in fear.

'I'm sorry,' Emma whispered into the space that the silence left behind.

Beth: Passwords

Beth remembered that she still had a back-up list of Emma's passwords. She'd given it her for safekeeping, just in case something happened to her or she couldn't get hold of her for some reason.

Well, that forward-thinking of Emma's turned out to be very useful. It was almost as if Emma had known something was going to happen. But that was Emma - she always had a plan for everything.

Scavenging around her room for the precious piece of paper, she found it eventually under a notebook. Typing in the main password that she found repeatedly circled, she soon had access to everything on Emma's phone.

Flicking through the phone as much as she could without the cracked screen posing an issue, she found old pictures of family holidays and pictures of both of them together on nights out.

Turning her attention to the text messages as a new one arrived, she scrolled through all of them and then clicked on the newest text.

'I'm sorry,'

The contact name at the top was a name that was extremely familiar to her.

Joe.

Pulling her bag onto her knee, Beth grabbed her phone and found his number. It was the same as the number on Emma's phone.

Alexis: The Favour

Alexis was soon awakened by the smell of tempting food downstairs. She was starving although she had eaten yesterday. She wasn't quite sure why they only ate breakfast, but she accepted it as normal.

Alexis was again wearing the mustard yellow crop top and obsidian black leggings. She walked downstairs again but her balance was slightly off. Perhaps something was wrong with her body, or maybe she was just tired.

Cole looked up at her as she entered the kitchen.

'We need to have a chat before we eat.'

His voice was icy-cold.

Alexis kept her eyes focused on the solid blackcurrant colour of the tablecloth in front of her.

What had she done?

Why did he want to talk to her?

All she could do was wait for the explosion of anger.

'Alexis, look at me,' Cole commanded in a soft voice.

Alexis did as she was told and raised her brown eyes to meet his grey ones, slowly and hesitantly.

'I need you to do me a favour.'

His voice was gentle and calm.

'Do you think you could do that for me?'

'What kind of favour?' Alexis asked in the same tone that Cole had used.

'I need you to collect something for me. It's quite simple really. It will only take five minutes,' he added with a warm, soothing smile.

'Sure,' Alexis agreed, not seeing any other option.

'You can start eating now, I'll go get some clothes together. Will you be okay on your own?' Cole touched her shoulder reassuringly.

Alexis nodded.

'You're doing the right thing, Alexis, I'm proud of you.' He left and Alexis's heart swelled with happiness, a grin fixed on her face while she ate and filled her glass to the brim with orange juice.

The Castle

'There is no need to be sorry. You didn't do all these horrible things to me,' Beth said, raising her head to look up at Emma.

'If I knew you before, I could've helped stop it.'

Beth shook her head and said nothing else in response.

Emma's head went up in alarm as she heard footsteps from outside the building and even Beth shared her look of alarm.

Emma paused for a few moments.

'Is there another way out of here?' she asked, keeping her voice low and her movements quiet.

Beth nodded, gesturing for her to get up and, with Emma's help, she began lifting the moth-eaten sofa, revealing a trap door underneath. It didn't make any sense to her whatsoever and it probably wouldn't even if Beth explained it. Acceptance was key.

'Are you coming?' Beth asked, lifting the trap door and positioning herself ready to climb through.

'Yes,' Emma whispered in reply, following her through.

Alexis: Nerves

Alexis soon finished eating and a million thoughts raced unstoppably through her head.

Was she prepared for this? She had to be.

Looking up as Cole entered the room, she took a sip from her glass of orange juice, not realising that her hand was shaking.

'I've put the clothes for later on your bed,' he told her. 'Just get dressed when you're finished up in here, okay?'

'Sure,' Alexis replied, submissive and obedient.

Going back to sit at the table, she carried on eating until she was finished.

'I guess I'll go and get ready now,' Alexis murmured to Cole and earned a nod.

'Can I use the bath?'

'If you make sure you wash it out afterwards.'

'I will,' Alexis replied. It was an attempt to demonstrate that she could obey orders and commands without hesitation.

Cole nodded.

'Go on then, but get changed afterwards,'

Alexis nodded in response and left the room.

After searching for what felt like hours, she found the upstairs bathroom. And the water, when she tested it, was boiling hot.

Slipping into the bath after running it, she decided to savour and remember the experience. After all, it may be the last bath she was able to have.

Closing her eyes, she sunk back into the water and tried to turn her mind off for a while.

It wouldn't be long until she would need to get prepped and dressed for whatever Cole wanted.

Beth: Could it be True?

Beth kept glancing at the phone number in disbelief, checking each digit. The guy she knew from college didn't seem like the type to get involved in Emma's kidnapping.

Soon she had received a few more texts from Michael about coursework but it was the texts he sent immediately afterwards that caught her eye:

'Got some more leads on the whole Emma disappearance thing. Saw you looking at the news articles when we met up last.

Let me help you.

M'

After the text there were a few links which she clicked on, unable to help her curiosity. The web pages showed very recent news articles about Emma's disappearance and they mentioned much of what the police knew so far.

Suddenly Michael had become extremely helpful to her rather than being a daily annoyance. It could become an interesting partnership.

Her phone went off again. Joe.

'Still on for tonight?'

If she asked him to tell her everything on the date tonight, would he? Hopefully, she would finally get the answers she wanted.

If Joe did have something to do with Emma's disappearance, she would need to find a way to get it out of him. But how?

Beth would a find a way.

She always did.

Alexis: Ready

A few hours later, she was standing by the doorway in her all-black outfit with thigh-high boots to match. All she had to do now was wait for Cole to tell her that they were ready to begin. Whatever it was.

'Ready?' Cole asked, appearing from nowhere.

'Yep, I'm ready.'

Alexis replied with a grin. It might hopefully hide the nerves.

'Good,' Cole smiled, and his voice radiated approval. As Cole left the house, Alexis followed.

She was ready for the task at hand.

The Castle

Somehow, Beth landed safely on the ground as did Emma, surprisingly.

Typically, Emma would have fallen flat on her face, likely due to unsuitable shoes, a heavy gown and the clumsiness gene buried deep within her.

Emma didn't recognise this part of the gardens. As if reading her mind, Beth spoke up.

'This is the other side of the palace gardens. People don't come up here much.'

'So, they won't find us?' Emma enquired with a slight frown.

'Not if we carry on walking.'

How she could Beth be so happy when there was a threat hanging over them? Emma had no clue.

'I'd say we have a couple of hours at most,' Beth added.

It was a guessing game as to which one of them the guards were looking for. And Beth's face indicated that she knew a lot more than she was letting on.

Beth: The 'Date'

Beth ran upstairs and frantically started getting herself sorted out for her date. She even ran the iron over her clothes as quickly as she could. Soon she was dressed in a long-sleeved navy-blue top with cut-out back and charcoal black leggings that were paired with the same navy-blue boots that matched her top.

She allowed her hair to fall down her back and shoulders in tousled waves. Taking a deep breath in, she stared at herself in the bathroom mirror.

Good.

She looked great. Attractive even.

Applying lip-gloss on her dry and chapped lips, Beth sorted out her bag, slung it across her shoulder and headed downstairs to wait for Joe.

Hearing a knock at the door, she jumped up, grabbing her keys and opening up. Joe was leaning against the doorway.

'Hey.'

He grinned at her approvingly.

'You look great,'

'Thanks,' Beth blushed, tucking her hair behind her ear. 'You too.'

'Let's go.'

Joe wrapped an arm around her shoulder as he led her to the car.

'Where are we going?' Beth asked.

'It's a surprise.'

Beth just grinned in response, though her mind was racing with millions of different thoughts. What were they going to talk about?

Beth reached towards the radio and turned the volume down completely. Joe looked at her.

'What's going on?' he asked.

'Stop the car for a minute.'

Joe pulled over into the nearest car park.

'What's up?'

Beth paused for a few moments.

'You knew Emma Winters.'

It was a statement. Not a question.

Joe frowned.

'I don't know Emma Winters.'

'Of course, you do! You sent her a text saying you were sorry about something!'

Joe's expression froze.

'I can explain!'

'Did you have something to do with her disappearance?'

Joe ran a hand through his hair and didn't meet her eyes, but then his hands attacked the steering wheel with sudden violence.

'Not in the way that you think.'

His voice was quiet - almost a strained whisper.

'I didn't kidnap her.'

'But you know who did?'

'Yes,' Joe admitted, casting his eyes to the floor. 'Yes, I do.'

Alexis: Discovery

She hadn't taken a single step outside the door before Cole grabbed her arm and yanked her inside the black car parked at the front of the house.

Wincing at the sunlight that was suddenly too bright for her to handle, Alexis sat up properly in the passenger seat and fumbled around with the seatbelt.

The car seemed familiar to her, but she couldn't place it. As its engine started up, she stared out the windows blankly, trying to see anything that wasn't a kaleidoscope of black shades, but she failed in her attempts.

She had no phone or watch on which to measure time, but she reckoned it must have been about an hour and a half before the car pulled to a halt. She shook off her unease and got out of the car slowly and carefully, staying steady while her eyes adjusted to the bright lights.

Was everything usually this bright?

A moment later, she heard another door slam shut from near her and turned to see that Cole was standing next to her, holding a pair of sunglasses. Slipping them on gratefully, she could finally see properly and turned around to see exactly where she was.

Alexis found herself in front of what looked like a college. Students talked excitedly and smoked cigarettes. They also played blaring music and she wanted to yell at them to make them stop.

She turned to Cole in annoyance, 'What exactly am I collecting?'

Alexis watched all of the students intently, until one of them locked eyes with her and rushed over, staring at her for signs of recognition.

'Emma?' he whispered; his face ghost white.

'You've been missing for months.'

'It's Michael. Don't you remember me?'

He took a few steps towards her, but Cole was behind her.

'You need to get him to leave with us,' his gruff voice commanded in her ear.

Alexis turned to Michael in response to Cole's commands.

'You need to come with us.'

She held out a hand for him to take.

The boy stopped, as Cole noticed his phone. He advanced towards him, grabbing the phone from his hands and throwing it to the floor.

'Come with us. Now,' he snarled,

Michael took Alexis's hand.

Alexis felt sick to the stomach.

She was collecting Michael?

This wasn't going to end well for anyone.

The Castle

Emma let out a pathetic wince as she felt her body freefalling. Goddamn, Beth. She did that on purpose. She must have.

Then Emma saw the guards scouting dangerously close to the tree where they were currently hiding. Thank God she had.

If they got caught...

Emma didn't want to think about that right now.

'What do we do' Beth mouthed.

They either needed defence or distraction.

Emma searched around in the bushes in a panic, and her hands clasped around something hard.

A rock.

Giving Beth a quick glance, she threw it away from their position, and the guards immediately followed.

'Come on!' Beth hissed impatiently in her ear.

The only option that they had was to run.

Alexis: Michael's Here

Now that they were all inside the house, Alexis could feel the tension brewing. It looked to be a typical domestic setting, but it clearly wasn't.

Alexis watched Cole as he got up and slammed the front door shut.

Flickering her eyes over towards Michael, she hoped he'd keep quiet. It looked as though he'd get it right. He had his eyes permanently glued to the floor and this gave Alexis the slightest bit of hope for his survival.

Cole glared at Alexis.

'Sit the fuck down. In there.' He snarled and pointed. Alexis obeyed.

Beth: You Know Who Took Emma?

Beth ran a trembling hand through her hair, not caring about their date anymore at all.

'You know who took Emma?'

Her voice was more of a whisper now. The realist that was beginning to set in was turning the blood in her veins stone cold. She shivered.

Joe only nodded, keeping his eyes glued to his hands,

'I'm sorry. If I could have stopped it, I would have done...'

'You could have stopped it!' Beth argued. 'You didn't have to help a twisted maniac who just wants to use Emma for God knows what!'

'You're wrong,' Joe replied, so softly that Beth struggled to hear him at first.

'What did you say?'

'I said you're wrong!' Joe snapped at her, his eyes flashing with anger, 'You think I would do this out of choice? Really?'

'I don't even know you!' Beth protested.

'Exactly, you don't know me.'

Beth's mind was working overtime. How and why could he work for a kidnapper?

Joe's eyes sprang up to hers as he sighed.

'Apparently he has my girlfriend stored away somewhere,' he began.

Beth nodded at him, prompting him to carry on talking.

'He's forced me to do a lot of things I never wanted to do. It was necessary to keep my girlfriend alive. If I didn't do it, I knew he would kill her.'

'We need to stop him.'

He nodded. 'We need to get back the people we love.'

The Castle

Emma slipped her hand into Beth's as they ran and started to pick up speed. Beth squeezed her hand tightly. Hearing nothing at all in the distance, they both assumed that they had outrun the guards. But even that didn't mean that they were safe.

They both stopped for a few minutes to catch their breath, and heard footsteps nearing them both.

'I've found her!' the guard yelled.

Emma swallowed nervously, anxiety running down her throat. Who were the guards chasing?

Whoever it was, Emma prepared herself to fight if she had to.

Beth: Where is Michael?

Beth woke the next morning to hear her phone blaring out a ringtone that she knew to be Michael's.

Unlocking her phone, she stared at the text and waited for the message to sink into her brain.

Emma is with some random guy.

Beth frantically rang Michael's number, but there was no reply, even after her fifth ring.

Strange.

Fear gripped her suddenly as she knew that he had been taken too.

Alexis: Innocent

Alexis watched Cole stride across the room. The man was full of anxiety and rage, like a ticking time bomb, and who knew when he would explode.

Alexis prepared herself for the worst as Cole glared at Michael with contempt in his eyes. What was going on? None of this made any sense.

The only thing that did make sense was to survive in the present. She had to make sure that Michael didn't get hurt. She didn't know why, but she knew she must protect him.

'Right,' Cole began. 'There are certain rules around here.'

Michael's head was still down, but Alexis nodded to show Cole that he had her full attention, and to save Michael from further danger.

'You're not allowed in each other's rooms without permission... You're not allowed to talk to each other without permission... Looks like one of you already broke that rule,'

He glared towards Michael whose head was still down.

'If you break those rules, you will be punished.'

Cole edged closer to Michael, and that's when it all happened. It began so quickly that nobody could have done anything to prevent it. Alexis could only watch as Michael endured a beating from Cole. Ruby red blood glistened around his mouth, covering his teeth and dripping slowly down his chin.

She had to watch, even when she heard a sickening crack coming from his body.

'There's a flannel and hot water in the kitchen. Clean up this mess before I come back.'

Then Cole stormed out of the house.

The Castle

It wasn't long before Emma and Beth had been marched back to the castle to await Cole's judgement.

But they both knew that Emma was going to be the only one to suffer. A million thoughts were running through Emma's mind about how exactly he was going to punish her this time.

It couldn't get worse than last night, could it?

As they walked through the corridors, Beth leaned over and whispered in Emma's ear.

'You need to kill him.'

'Kill who?'.

'Cole.'

The thought hadn't occurred to her before. She knew she didn't have the guts.

They had soon been pushed into the throne room. Somehow Beth had managed to remain upright, but Emma was on her knees in front of Cole. Like robots following orders programmed into their systems.

'Emma.'

Cole greeted her and rose from his comfortable position in his throne.

'My lord,' Emma said, looking up at him and giving him a half-hearted mock bow.

Of course, a huge part of her was terrified of him, but her feelings of hate were even stronger. Cole was trying to prove that he still had power over her, so Emma must play pretend. Let him live the illusion, believing that he still had control, but Emma wasn't planning to submit that easily. Not anymore.

'You were so much better when you were

gagged.'

Emma's eyes slid to Beth. No! A guard was behind her, and a knife pressed to the back of her throat.

'Let Beth go,' Emma shouted.

'Oh no,' Cole smirked. 'That's not going to happen. You broke the rules. You went out without permission.'

He was moving closer now.

'That's not Beth's fault!' Emma protested, and suddenly felt a hard and stinging slap on her face.

'I wasn't aware I had to ask permission, sire,' she said, her voice sharp-edged.

Emma watched as Cole gritted his teeth and clenched both of his fists tightly.

'Guards, escort Miss Winters out. I'll deal with her later.'

Emma saw the guard press the knife harder against Beth's throat.

A mixture of panic and anger rose up in Emma's own throat at his next words.

'I'll deal with her friend in her absence.'

Cole's icy cold eyes turned onto Beth as he gave a sick and twisted grin.

Beth: Contacting Zoey

When Beth had eventually calmed her mind, she began to think a little more methodically.

Michael never ignored her - not unless there was something going on. Deep down, she knew that her gut instincts were right, and that he was in trouble.

She sent Joe a message.

'We need to talk. Something's happened.
I need you.
Now.'

Grabbing Emma's phone, Beth began to flick through her Facebook account to find Zoey and Mia on Emma's friends list. Which one was Emma closest to?

Going back to the home screen of Emma's phone, it was soon obvious that Zoey was close, but Mia, inexplicably, seemed to hate her.

Returning to her laptop, Beth began to compose a Facebook message for them both. Maybe they wouldn't reply but it had to be worth a shot.

Hi,
I'm Beth, one of Emma's ex-friends and I'm looking into Emma's disappearance. I want to find out who has taken her and get her home safely. Message me if you're interested in meeting up and having a chat.'

She pressed the send button. Now, she just needed a response.

Alexis: Blood

Alexis glanced timidly at Michael who was sprawled out on the floor. A small pool of blood had been growing, fed by the lip that had been bleeding continuously since Cole had attacked him.

'Shit,' Alexis muttered under her breath.

Michael looked at her in a brief acknowledgement. His eyes pleaded for help and Alexis didn't blame him.

But if she helped him, Cole would hurt the both of them. But Cole wasn't with them. And he had ordered her to clean up all the blood.

Alexis was going to take a risk.

'I'll be back in a minute.'

Alexis walked into the kitchen and grabbed a bucket from the counter top. Filling it with hot water, she scanned around in the cupboards under the sink to find a cloth.

With bucket and cloth, she reached Michael and knelt next to him.

'I'm going to clean you up, okay?'

'Okay,'

'You've been missing for a while now,' Michael said as he winced from the pain.

'No, I haven't. I don't know what you're talking about.'

'Emma, what has he done to you?'

'My name is Alexis, and he hasn't done anything to me.'

She squeezed the flannel in the water and scrubbed the floor until her arms ached.

Making sure that the floor was clean of any blood, she headed out with the bucket. Michael closed his eyes.

Beth: Message from Zoey

Emma and Michael were still missing, without a trace and even the police hadn't been able to trace them. They'd had a sighting but couldn't prove the identity of the people seen.

Joe had called Beth earlier. They were going to work on their problem together.

Meanwhile Beth checked her Facebook account and saw the message in her inbox.

It was from Zoey.

Opening the message up, she sat in front of her phone and read.

'I'd be happy to meet up with you, how about meeting at the Black Cat café at around half 11?'

Beth would have to skip college, but this was more important. Anyway, her mum would never have to know, and she was well up to date with her work.

Ignoring the pang of guilt she felt, Beth typed a quick and simple response:

'Sure. See you there.'

Maybe none of this would have happened if they had taken that extra bit of care of Emma. It was hard not to apportion blame, but Beth tried to calm as she got into the bath. This meeting could change everything.

The Castle

Pacing around her room nervously, Emma let her worry consume her completely. What the hell was he doing to Beth in there?

Of course, this was just another one of Cole's power games. He loved to prove to her how far he was prepared to go. She jumped as she heard her door unlock and open with painful slowness.

Readying herself to fight and protect herself against an intruder, Emma calmed immediately when she saw her visitor. Michael spoke.

'I'm not supposed to be here, but we need to talk.' His tone was urgent, and this was matched by his panicked looks and the promptness of him shutting the door.

'What is it?'

'It's about Beth. Cole's put her in the cells. She isn't in a good way, Emma,'

She ran a hand through her hair.

'I'm going to get her out,' she said, and she intended to keep it, no matter what.

Beth: Meeting with Zoey

Beth had opted for her thigh-high boots, but unlike her usual ankle boots, these were noisy and clicked against the pavement.

She reached the café, still unsure whether this was a wise idea. What if this was a trap or some kind of a joke? Beth hoped not but kept the thought in her head as she made her way inside.

She tried to suppress a smile as she glanced around at the café's black and white theme. All the tables were decorated with some variation of black and white blocks. Even some of the sofas were half black and half white.

Brushing off the thought of the creepy clack cat clock she'd just noticed, Beth began surveying the busy room and wondering which of the customers was Zoey. A blonde girl had isolated herself in the corner. A beanie and a long choppy fringe covered much of her face.

'You must be Zoey,' Beth said as she headed over to sit opposite her.

'Yeah, that's me.'

She removed her beanie and took a sip of her hot chocolate.

'So, you got my email?'

'Yeah. So, you're looking for Emma?' Zoey's shoulders pushed back against the chair.

'Yep, I am.'

Beth couldn't help the coldness and beginnings of anger. If Emma meant anything to her friends, then why weren't they looking for her too?

'Can you tell me what happened that night?'

Beth's question earned a sigh from Zoey.

'Emma went off with Joe, we all got into an argument and Mia and I just left.'

'You just left your best friend with a random guy you didn't know? What the fuck?' Beth snapped angrily, eyes blazing.

Zoey sighed. 'I can't talk to you anymore.'

Beth watched as she stormed out without another word.

Alexis: Cole's Room

Alexis emptied the bucket and rinsed out the flannel before putting everything back exactly as it had been before.

She headed upstairs after checking up on Michael who was sleeping quite peacefully.

Oddly, some of the doors were wide open, as if in a personal invitation to look round.

One she knew to be Cole's room. Alexis knew it was wrong and that it was an invasion of his privacy, but curiosity got the better of her.

A double bed with black and white patterned duvet was placed jutting into the middle of the room, pushed against a back wall. Along the same wall were three black chests of drawers, blocking the window.

Opening a drawer, she found photos of herself. Ones she'd seen before, on her own wall. Looking further down, she found a dull orange folder with the name 'Emma' scrawled on the front in capital letters.

Whoever 'Emma' was, she must have been important. For once she managed to fight against the curiosity infecting her brain. She put the folder back and left the room exactly how it had been.

Before she managed to leave the room, Alexis noticed something that made her stop in her tracks. She shivered. The photo was of a young woman staring blankly into the camera, and the photo's main focus was her bruised and battered face. The girl's dark hair was not unlike her own. In fact, it was eerily similar. Was she being turned into this girl in front of her?

Moving her fingers from the bottom of the photo, she saw a name written in heavy-handed capital letters.

Maisie.

The writer of the note. Surely, it must be.

Then she noticed something else. A red cross in the corner of the photo. And Alexis knew that Maisie was no longer alive.

Beth: Tension

As Beth watched Zoey get up and walk out, she was hit with confusion.

Why would one of Emma's supposed best friends not be willing to give her information that would help find her?

Could she be hiding something?

God, was that even Zoey after all? For all Beth knew, she could have been an imposter posing as Emma's friend. This was another thing she would need to talk to Joe about.

In the middle of a quiet and awkward dinner, Beth's mother began to talk. She didn't talk much, and when she did, it was usually pretty serious. What could it possibly be this time?

'Your college grades are slipping,' Beth's mum started.

Beth knew where this was going. It would be yet another lecture about college and how she needed to put more effort in. She would say that even though her best friend was missing she needed to stay focused. She remained silent.

Noticing her silence, her mother continued.

'You've fallen down in a few units recently, which you know will affect your university opportunities.'

Beth shrugged inwardly. It didn't matter. All her thoughts had been taken up on other matters.

'I don't know if I want to go anymore,' Beth admitted, slightly scared and nervous about how her mother would react.

'What do you mean, you don't want to go anymore? Is this because of Emma?'

'Everything isn't about fucking Emma!' Beth

screamed. For a long while she had felt the anger bubbling up inside her.

That was when her phone went off, breaking the tension. She picked it up and glanced at the text, knowing exactly who had sent it.

'Park in five minutes?'

'Is that Michael?' her mum asked.

'Yeah,' Beth lied. She got up, put on her shoes, and left the house.

Hearing a sudden noise, Beth was startled to hear a chime coming from her hands. It was a message from Zoey.

'I'm sorry I stormed out earlier. The whole thing is just a lot to deal with. Are you OK?"

Sighing heavily, Beth continued walking and ignored the message lingering on her phone. Zoey was probably waiting for an instant response, but she could wait.

Alexis: More Paints

Cole was standing in the doorway surrounded by shopping bags when Emma found her way downstairs.

'I bought some food,' Cole announced, making his way into the kitchen with all of the carrier bags. The announcement of food made Michael peer up from his position on the sofa. He was looking a little better.

Alexis stepped to one side, ensuring that she was completely out of Cole's way. She moved over nearer to the still-silent Michael.

After a few moments of hesitation, she followed Cole into the kitchen and started to help out with putting away the contents of the carrier bags.

'Alexis, I got you some more paints just in case.' Cole winked at her, passing her the pack of paints that he had pulled out of one of the few bags that were left.

'Thanks.' She gave him a bright smile.

'Do you mind if I help with dinner?'

'Sure, that would be great. Go and put your stuff upstairs and we can start.'

He smiled at her as she went out of the room and back upstairs like an obedient child.

She couldn't hear what Cole said to Michael as she went upstairs.

The Castle

'It's not your fault,' Michael whispered.

'But it is,' Emma replied, quietly.

'Can I do anything to help?' Michael asked.

No, she couldn't allow another good person to get hurt. Michael couldn't get involved.

'I could create a distraction so you can get into the cells,' he suggested.

Emma paused. It might work, if the distraction was big enough.

'Fine. But you stay in the shadows, out of sight.'

'Agreed.'

Michael held out a hand for her to shake and she smiled, taking his hand, shaking it and sealing the deal.

'I'll see you later then.'

Emma decided to change out of the gown she wore in the gardens and into something more practical. She would likely need it for later. The option to do nothing was no longer available. She had to push herself and save her friend.

Alexis: Dinner Preparation

'Everything is ready and waiting,' Cole said.

'Great.'

Alexis scanned the kitchen. Everything they'd need was already spread out on the counters.

But why was Michael in here?

'Michael is going to help you cook, I'll be back in a bit to check on your progress.'

He left.

Alexis grabbed a knife and began cutting up the peppers while Michael put the mince in the microwave to defrost.

'Look, I'm sorry about being weird earlier,' Michael sighed, avoiding eye contact.

There was no reply from Alexis as she carried on cutting the peppers, only narrowly missing cutting her fingers.

'Alexis,' Michael started but he stopped when she glared at him.

'I don't accept your apology,' she snapped in response. The cooking continued in silence.

Beth: Descent

Beth headed fearlessly into the pitch-black outside, coat on and phone in pocket. The park was only five minutes away.

All she had to do was meet Joe. They would talk about their next steps and then could put everything in motion, and it would all work out fine. That was what she hoped, anyway. Her mind was racing with all the potential outcomes.

Entering the park, she pulled up her jacket's hood. Suddenly, Beth felt hands wrap around her waist from behind and her whole body urged her to fight back against whatever threat was attempting to drag her down against her will.

'What the fuck are you doing? It's me, Beth. It's Joe. Jesus Christ.'

Beth spun around.

'Shit, sorry.' Beth ran her hands through her hair and gave Joe an apologetic glance.

'Were you expecting anyone else?' Joe joked, with a slight chuckle.

Beth glared. 'It's not funny!'

They began to walk.

'We need to sort out a plan for how we're going to get everyone back,' Joe said, his voice suddenly deathly serious.

'Right.'

They reached a bench and sat together, staring into the darkness.

'So how should we do it?' Beth asked, looking up at Joe.

'I know one of Cole's hideout places. He might have taken them there, but it would mean me going away for few day.'

Joe looked down at the floor.

'Do you have to? What's to stop you from going back to him and helping him take more people?'

'You'll have to trust me.'

'Fine,' Beth replied reluctantly, realising that her only other option was to do this alone.

'If you don't come back in those two days, I will kill you.'

'I know,' Joe replied, turning away from her. 'I'll leave in the morning.'

Alexis: Silence

Within an hour, Alexis and Michael had finished the food prep and had begun to cook. Most of the work had been done.

That was when Cole popped his head around the door, checking up on them just as he'd promised.

'Is the food ready yet? I'm starving.'

'Not yet, give it another hour and it'll be done.'

Alexis was desperate to appease the anger she could see slowly emerging. All Cole did was nod and leave the room.

The tension brewed over the kitchen's two silent figures.

The Castle

Emma's new dress was sleek and coal-black. It was her most practical gown when it came to movement and invisibility.

Michael and Emma had planned to break Beth out of the cells, but Emma hadn't been told about Michael's plans to make a distraction.

But one thing that she was certain of - she wouldn't be grovelling to Cole for Beth's release. He'd only want something in return, and she had a feeling that he'd want more than Emma was able to give.

Michael showed up at the agreed time.

'Are you ready?' Emma asked.

He nodded, 'As ready as I can be.'

Taking a deep breath, Emma followed Michael, who was hiding in the shadows, down into the cells.

Michael Isn't Eating Tonight

Dinner was cooked, and Alexis was helping Michael set the table correctly. Both knew Cole would check up on them soon.

Lighting the candles and smiling at their handiwork, Alexis heard the door creak open and assumed it was Cole. It was.

'I'm just about to start serving up food if you want to sit down.'

Alexis gestured to the table that she and Michael had perfected. The candles made the perfect finishing touch.

'Michael isn't eating tonight,' Cole said.

'What do you mean he isn't eating tonight? We've already set the table for three.'

'I mean precisely what I said. Michael can go upstairs.'

He made a hand gesture as if to shoo Michael out of the room. Was starving him really necessary when Michael had already been through enough? Alexis cast her eyes over to Michael, willing him to comply, and watched as he followed orders and headed upstairs. At least he would be safe that night. Alexis didn't know if she was.

'How about we just have the night to ourselves then?' Cole suggested.

'Sure,' Alexis replied, her heart racing.

Cole smiled and sank down in a seat, seeming to be occupied with his thoughts.

'Oh, we don't have any drink. Let me go get some,' he said, suddenly rising and disappearing into the kitchen. Cole soon emerged juggling two champagne glasses and a tall bottle in his hands. After setting them down on the table, he returned to the kitchen.

Beth: Truth

Only a few days had passed since Joe had left, maybe for good, and Beth wasn't sure when he was going to show his face again.

College had been lonely without him to talk to. It wasn't just lonely. It was unimportant.

All that mattered was finding Emma.

Alexis: In Love

Eventually dinner came to an end, and as Alexis finished the washing up, she stepped back to admire the kitchen.

It still looked messy, but she guessed that was a sign that the night had gone well.

She wasn't aware that Cole was leaning against the wall watching her. Well, not until he sneaked up behind her and wrapped his arms around her waist in an embrace.

'What are you doing?' Alexis squealed, bright red patches forming on her cheeks.

'Hugging you.'

Alexis blushed, unsure of how she should react, especially when Cole's hands moved down her waist. Then he spun her around and kissed her. From what she could remember, that was the best kiss she had experienced in a long time.

Alexis stirred and worked on waking up completely, but she didn't want to leave the warm confines of the bed. She didn't remember much of last night apart from dinner with Cole.

Rubbing her eyes a few times, a sudden realisation hit her. She was in Cole's bedroom and she was naked. Cole was lying naked next to her.

Alexis suddenly remembered all of what happened and smiled. Getting out of bed, she put on a top she'd discovered on the floor.

What happened to her clothes? Surely, they should be around here somewhere.

From the other side of the bed, Cole began to wake up.

'Hey.'

Alexis moved over to his side.

'Morning.'

'Sleep well?' Alexis asked.

'Really well,' he smirked and the look he gave her turned her cheeks a scarlet red.

'You?'

'I slept well too,' Alexis giggled, and her cheeks became hot from her blushing.

Cole leaned in and kissed her, and Alexis welcomed the embrace.

'I should get up,' Alexis whispered, only to be pulled back down onto the bed.

'I'm going to make breakfast,' Alexis insisted. 'I want to do something nice for you.'

Cole raised an eyebrow at the girl in front of him and watched as she left the room.

Alexis made a beeline for the kitchen where she found Michael hovering around the kettle. Anger filled her suddenly. That job was her job, not his.

'I can take it from here,' she said coldly and shoved him out of the way.

Alexis flicked the kettle on and waited for it to boil, getting two mugs out of the cupboard and setting them down on the counter. While she was lingering by the kettle, she took some bread and slipped it into the toaster.

Glancing over at Michael, she noticed him eating away at something discreetly. How had he managed to sneak something in?

Was it something he already had in his bag?

Sighing heavily at him for going against Cole, Alexis returned to what she had been doing.

'He's using you,' Michael said, staring at her from his position by the sink.

'He has a name,' Alexis glared.

She sorted out the tea and coffee as she heard the kettle finish boiling.

'He's not using me,' she added, trying her best to remain calm.

'Cole is your captor and nothing else.'

'Here you go again, making up weird stories that don't make any sense!' Alexis took a gulp of her tea.

'We slept together,' she announced.

'That doesn't mean he loves you.'

'I bet you've never been in love, so how would you know?' Alexis spat.

Putting the toast on a plate, Alexis turned to see her Cole in the doorway.

'Is everything alright in here? I thought I heard raised voices.'

He gave them both a piercing glare, but Alexis knew it was for affect. He wasn't really mad.

'Everything is fine,' Alexis insisted, just a little shakily.

Cole glanced at the coffee and toast in her hands and grinned at her.

'Thanks for breakfast. We're going out in about ten minutes, so hurry up and get dressed.'

Michael opened his mouth to speak but Cole cut him off.

'Not you. Just Alexis.'

He gave Cole a look of disgust before leaving the room.

'Still think he's amazing?' Michael questioned as she stormed out after Cole, with her tea mug in her hand.

The Castle

Emma headed down the steep steps of the cells slowly. She blended in quite easily with the surrounding darkness, just as Michael did.

Looking over at his figure, she realised that he almost blended in too well. It seemed as if he'd perhaps even done this before.

Their only sources of light were the dimly lit torches that cast shadows along the stone wall. They led to two guards standing in front of the cell entrance.

Emma's hands began to shake and her body to sweat. She had to calm down and do it quickly - before she gave everything away.

As she moved closer, she could see a grey rack built into the stone wall. On it a group of keys hung carelessly close and within reach.

Michael had already slipped away so Emma headed over to the guards. 'I'm here to see a prisoner,' she announced.

'Which one?' the guard asked in a gruff voice.

'Beth.'

'She isn't permitted any visitors.'

'But...' Emma protested. Their glares made her stumble and falter.

Just as she was turning back towards the corridor that allowed her to leave the cells, a servant girl came running past and knocking into her. She couldn't hear what the girl was saying but the guards seemed to disapprove, and they ran after her. Emma saw her chance, strolled over casually to the rack and snatched the keys.

Hopefully one would fit the lock of Beth's cell.

Beth: Park

Tapping her fingers against the desk, she was becoming impatient, waiting for her last lesson to end.

Why hadn't Joe messaged her back?

His absence filled her with anxiety. Was he hurt?

As soon as her lesson ended, she made her way home. About to step into the house as she unlocked the front door, her phone buzzed suddenly.

'Don't go home right now.
Park.'

Alexis: Bowling

Alexis put on her shoes on and slipped a jacket over the top of her outfit. It had been carelessly left on the floor, but it fit her nicely which was a bonus.

'Alright?' Cole asked her.

Alexis nodded in response.

'I thought we could have a proper day out with each other. Like people do,' Cole grinned, obviously in good spirits.

'Really?'

This wasn't a flippant response. She was genuinely surprised as there was still tension hanging freely between them. Alexis hadn't asked him the question that she had wanted to for a long time: about why he had taken her in after the death of her parents. Perhaps she would get the chance to ask him today?

'Mmm.'

Once in the car, Cole turned the radio on to the news station. Suddenly he stiffened up at the name, Emma, and flipped the station to a generic pop music one. Alexis wished she could have heard more about what happened to the girl, as curiosity had her in its grip, but she forced herself to let go.

She stared out of the window and closed her eyes as wind brushed against her face and caressed her hair. The outside was bright, with a beautiful array of colours everywhere, helped by the shining sun and the sky's rich shade of blue.

Everything was going to go well. She just knew it.

Beth: Into the Car

Entering the park hesitantly, Beth could hear the creaking of a swing as it moved with the wind - slow yet full of purpose. One silvery-grey swing moved alone.

She hoped that Joe would arrive soon. She was freezing even with a coat on and if there was someone lurking around watching her, she had few means of defending herself. Cold hands reaching into her pockets, she pulled out her phone instantly and hovered over the call button on Joe's name.

It was soon after that she heard her name being called from the opposite side of the park.

'Beth!' the familiar voice yelled.

This version of Joe walking towards her had bruises all over his face.

'What?' Beth started, but was promptly cut off by Joe's arm dragging her small frame out of the park and towards a rusty grey car.

The Castle

Aware that she was running on borrowed time that she didn't have much of at all, Emma frantically running through the gate and tried to unlock the cell.

Each key slipped from her hand in turn, until she was only left with one. But it seemed way too small for the lock.

Turning the key in the lock, she heard a click and grinned to herself.

Yes! She'd done it!

Pushing Beth's cell door open, she heard movement from behind her, relaxing as she realised that it was only a flushed-looking Michael.

'You have twenty minutes at a guess.'

'Right,' Emma replied and began searching for Beth in the darkness.

'Michael, can you put the keys back?'

Emma watched as Michael moved to the rack.

'Beth?' she called into the cell. 'It's me. It's Emma.'

Emma saw a shadow move from within the cell. It was a figure that looked vaguely like the Beth she knew. A shadow of it, perhaps.

'Trust me?' Emma said, holding out a hand for her to take.

'Yes.'

Beth: In Hiding

'Get in the car,' Joe ordered.

'I'll explain on our way there,' he added in a slightly gentler tone, and they set off in awkward silence. There was no way that Beth was going to break it.

'I met with the guy that took Emma and Michael,' Joe finally said as soon as they were away from the park.

Beth went deathly silent. She had to remind herself that Joe was working with her. Not against her.

'And?'

'He was pissed at me,' Joe admitted.

'Why?'

'Because he knows people have been looking into Emma's disappearance.'

Joe gave her a dark look.

'Why would he be pissed at you for that?'

Joe stopped the car at a set of traffic lights and turned to look at Beth.

'Because I haven't... dealt with the problem.'

Beth looked away, feeling sick to the stomach and pushing down the taste of bile from her mouth.

She wondered how many other people would need to be... dealt with...

It didn't make her feel any better.

'You can't go home,' he said.

'Well where am I going to stay, then?'

'At a hotel, with me,' Joe replied, as if it was obvious.

Alexis: Bowling

It wasn't long before the car pulled up outside a brightly-coloured building. Neon lights flashed promoting free games if you booked two rounds. They were at a bowling alley.

Alexis felt a smile creeping up onto her lips as she saw families together, all laughing and joking around with each other. But the vision set something else off within her too.

Alexis was surprised that Cole had even decided to let her out. Normally his rules were quite strict, and she'd no idea of what suddenly made him change his mind. Something must have happened, but what?

Cole came up behind her and enveloped her in his arms. 'What's wrong?' he asked.

Alexis glanced at Cole.

'I'm fine. Honestly.'

She tried her best to brush away her emotions, but the hint of sadness in her voice betrayed her. She knew that her stare towards the families told Cole everything he needed to know.

Together, they headed into the building and towards the bowling alley that Cole had booked. They exchanged their shoes for bowling pairs and went over to the lane, where food and drinks were already waiting.

Alexis's first game was going well. Strikes on every turn.

'Damn, you're good at bowling,' Cole muttered, in annoyance.

Alexis grinned and took another sip of her drink and a bite out of her hotdog.

'Good luck,' she teased as he threw a bowling ball down into their lane.

That was when a stranger glanced over in their direction.

'Oh my God, it's Emma Winters. Someone call the police!'

Alexis wanted to explain that she wasn't this Emma person but before she could, Cole had grabbed her and pulled her out of the alley and back to the car.

Alexis: Realisation

He didn't speak to Alexis for the whole journey home, being too busy picking up speed in the car.

'For fuck's sake,' Cole snarled and hit the steering wheel as they returned to the house.

Alexis had no opportunity to say or do anything in response as she was immediately dragged inside the house by her wrist. Michael jumped up when he saw them.

'What are you doing?' he demanded, following them as Cole dragged Emma into a room.

'You're coming with us this time,' Cole snarled, clamping his other hand around Michael's wrist.

Alexis cried out in pain as she was thrown to the floor face-first, as was Michael.

The room had walls of obsidian black. A chair in the corner had chains and handcuffs dangling from the arms.

Why did she feel like she had seen this before?

Cole grinned. Somehow, she knew exactly what was coming.

Beth: Hotel

Going to a hotel with Joe?

It seemed to be a done deal, though Beth was apprehensive about how the whole thing was going to pan out.

Joe tapped his fingers against the steering wheel impatiently. Beth wished she knew what was going on in his head.

'Can you tell me more about Emma's captor?'

She watched Joe, but her didn't take his eyes off the road.

'Later. When we know that it's safe.'

After a few hours of what Beth considered to be aimless driving, they pulled up in front of a hotel.

'Come on,' Joe urged, grabbing his jacket and opening the car door. Unquestioningly, Beth soon followed suit, doing following him into the hotel.

Joe went straight to the desk and chatted to the receptionist. Glancing around, Beth noticed how run-down the hotel was. Inexplicably, that made her feel better.

Joe presented her with a room key.

'First floor,' he muttered.

Alexis: The Chair

'Get in the chair, Alexis,' Cole ordered.

'Why are you doing this?' she asked in a desperate whisper.

'I have to keep both of you somewhere they can't find you.' As if it was a casual and everyday occurrence.

In the blink of an eye, Cole had picked Alexis up, forced her into the chair, and handcuffed her tightly.

Tears began to fall down Alexis's face and Cole wiped them away.

'I'm only doing this to keep you safe.'

Michael watched from the corner. Powerless.

Alexis nodded.

'I understand.'

She tried not to struggle against her restraints as she knew it would only make everything worse.

Cole then turned to Michael and grinned.

Alexis knew that he was going to have fun torturing Michael, and she hated him for it.

The Castle

Michael checked that the area around them was safe and that nobody was around, Emma held on tightly to Beth's hand as they darted out of the cell. All was quiet.

Soon they arrived at her chambers and Emma could finally see Beth properly. Her dress was hanging from her body, completely torn, and her hair looked a mess and as if somebody had tried to pull all of it out.

But that wasn't the worst thing, Emma was more shocked about the number of purple and black bruises on her friend's body and face. Wrapping a supportive arm around Beth, she led her to sit down, made her a hot drink and went to run her a hot bath.

'Emma?' Beth asked suddenly in a whisper.

Emma glanced up suddenly, 'Yeah?'

'Promise me you'll kill him.'

'I promise,' Emma replied seriously.

Taking a deep breath, she got onto her knees and scanned underneath her bed. Moving the loose floorboard, she found her violet coloured notebook and grinned to herself.

Yes. Her book of ideas was still here. Emma was going to do this for Beth.

Alexis: Chained

That was when it suddenly hit her. Cole had tied Alexis up first to ensure she didn't interfere with what Cole was going to do to Michael.

She had been forced into a static front-row seat.

Cole approached Michael and wrapped chains around his waist and arms, then proceeded to apply shackles to his ankles. He obviously couldn't move much. In comparison to him, Alexis's restraints were positively liberating.

They both watched as Cole chuckled then left the room.

Beth: Safe

As Beth climbed the steep stairs with Joe, her mind was completely blank.

Their room's door seemed to have previously been pulled off of its hinges. This was quite a rundown place. Beth winced as they entered. The wallpaper was peeled halfway down the wall, flaky and pretty much destroyed as could be seen by most of the pickings in heaps on the floor.

She knew that most of what the room provided would either be dirty or broken.

Beth let out a groan and collapsed on her bed.

'What?' Joe asked, an eyebrow raised at her.

'How long are we staying here?'

'Only tonight,' Joe replied, seriousness in his tone. 'We're leaving for Cole's place tomorrow,'

'Cole?' Beth's head perked up at the new name.

'Emma and Michael's captor,' he replied quietly, not giving anything away on his face. 'And...'

He paused before continuing.

'...And the other girl. Maisie. But I never did find out what happened to her.'

Beth spoke.

'It's late, we should sleep.'

'Yeah. Night then.'

'Night.'

Beth ignored her buzzing phone and fell into a deep sleep.

The Castle

Whilst Beth was busy in the bath, Emma began to flick through her notebook. She was surprised that Cole hadn't found it yet.

Its contents were simple: lists of ways to kill him, some of them circled.

Emma grinned to herself as she discovered an idea that could be easy to pull off - even for her...

Slamming the notebook shut, her decision was made. Emma got up, shouting into the bathroom to let Beth know that she was going out.

It was time to put her plan in action.

Alexis: Proof

'I have to tell you something,' Michael announced.

Alexis looked up from her restraints.

'If this is about me being that Emma person...' She trailed off, sighing irritably and getting ready for another argument.

'I have proof,' he replied, a serious look in his eyes. 'You need to trust me, Emma,'

'What kind of proof?'

'A newspaper article. Look, you need to trust me. It's the only way that we can get out of here.'

'How?' Alexis asked curiously, 'We're both restrained, and we can't do anything about it.'

'I might have something in my pockets, if I can reach them.'

A few attempts gave him access.

'Would a paperclip work?' he asked hopefully.

'It might.'

After fifteen minutes, he had managed to move his hand close to his ankle shackles, paperclip in his hand as he reached the lock. He managed to unlock them within just a few minutes, and both of them breathed a sigh of relief.

'Okay, now use your feet to pass the paperclip over to me,' Alexis instructed, and Michael obeyed.

Managing to grasp the paperclip under her foot, she screamed in pain as she made a slow move to grab and hold it securely in her hands.

'Are you okay?'

'Yeah,' Alexis replied, gritting her teeth at the fiery pain spreading up her arm.

Managing to unlock her arms, she did the same to her ankles and stood up shakily. All of her movements felt unsure, her head was spinning, and her arms ached.

Ignoring the searing pain her arm, she trudged over to Michael, 'Where was that proof?'

He made a gesture towards the article carefully folded in his pocket, and then towards a mirror.

'Look,' he said.

And there was the proof she needed.

Alexis was Emma.

She felt like she was going to be violently sick.

Cole had been lying to Emma this entire time.

Emma leaned down to kiss Michael's cheek, 'Thank you,' she whispered.

Michael smiled up at her.

'No problem, Emma,'

Alexis returned the smile, but it quickly faded as she saw Cole standing by the door.

The Castle

The trek to the physician's court was a lot quicker than usual, likely because she was focused entirely on her goal.

Making sure that it seemed as if she had a severe pain coming from her chest, she raised her hand to the door and knocked. Emma pretended to grimace in pain as the door creaked open.

'My lady?' came the physician's scared voice.

'Sorry,' Emma whispered. 'I wouldn't have come, but I'm in a lot of pain.'

'Come in, come in... Whatever is the matter?' he asked, with genuine worry in his voice.

'Really bad chest pain,' Emma managed.

'Is it your ribs?' he asked her., 'I know they were giving you a lot of pain.'

Emma paused.

'Yes, they still are.' It was no lie.

'I'll go make you up some more solutions.' With that, the physician disappeared into another room and Emma began her search.

Picking up a footstall that she found in the corner of the room, she began searching the shelves. It wasn't long before she found the very thing she wanted.

Crushed belladonna.

She pocketed it just as the physician came back. The vials of liquid she needed had been placed in a wicker basket.

She thanked him, said her goodbyes and headed back to the castle.

Emma: Sacrifice

Emma heard a gunshot and froze, knowing exactly what had happened to Michael.

He was dead, and it was because of her.

Sobs ripped through Emma's body as she curled up in a ball. First her identity had been snatched away from her, and now Michael was going to die, and it was all because she hadn't believed him.

Cole would pay for this.

Her eyes flickered over to the side table where she knew Cole's lighter was and slipped it into her pocket. She would need it later.

Hearing footsteps, she whipped her head around to face the figure standing there that she knew was Cole.

'I had to do it, Alexis. He was dangerous.'

His voice was low as he approached her to wipe the tears from her face.

Emma had to play along for now, as she knew it was her only chance of survival.

Both Emma and Alexis had to collide into one person. It was the only way.

'I know,' Emma responded quietly.

'We should both go to bed and get some sleep. We can clean everything up in the morning.'

He touched her on the small of her back and they both headed upstairs.

Beth: Cole's House

They were up and out of the hotel as quick as they could be the next morning. Beth felt mucky and disorientated but that didn't matter much.

'How long until we get there?'

'A few hours,' Joe replied, silent and brooding. It seemed usual for him, so she decided not to question it. Instead she turned up the music playing on the radio. It helped a little to fill the awkward silence between them.

An eternity seemed to have passed when they eventually pulled up outside the place where Emma and Michael were supposedly being held.

When they were both out of the car, Beth glanced around at her surroundings. She had expected a remote location, but this was a normal neighbourhood - kids were playing out the front and she could hear a couple arguing.

Beth gave Joe a questioning look. His features changed almost instantly as he stared towards one of the windows.

'Call the police and the fire brigade,' Joe whispered.

Beth nodded, eyes widening as she followed his gaze, and her hands fumbled with her phone.

Emma: Craving

As soon as she made sure Cole was definitely asleep, Emma had sneaked out of bed and pulled the lighter from the pocket of her jeans.

There was only one way for this to end.

She couldn't let him live. She also couldn't leave this house and survive in the real world.

She sparked up the lighter, held it under a magazine, and waited for the fire to begin.

Maybe smoke inhalation would finish her off.

Watching as the flames rose, she hoped the flames would increase quickly.

Emma needed to die.

She craved it.

The smoke began to kick in and Emma started coughing. It wasn't long before everything turned to nothing.

Beth: Rescue

When the fire brigade and ambulance turned up, Beth was pacing anxiously as they charged inside.

What if there was nothing they could do to help Emma? What if she was already dead?

Beth stared at the window. The flickers of orange flames were less intense now. The fire brigade was doing their job. And medics flooded from the waiting ambulance as soon as they were given the all clear.

Police sirens neared and paramedics carried out the bruised and burned figure of Emma, strapped down to a stretcher, with an oxygen mask over her face.

She suppressed the panic rising within her.

'Miss? Are you okay?' a police officer asked her. It was one she recognised from her mother's interview.

'Is she going to be okay?' her voice came in a shaky whisper.

'I'm sure they'll look after her and get her back to normal.'

With that, the officer headed into the building with the rest of the team.

Beth glanced at Joe, worry in her eyes.

This wasn't over yet.

As Beth looked over at the firemen, one of them was shouting triumphantly about something they'd found on the floor, and his eyes were glistening with what seemed to be a twisted form of excitement.

They shouldn't have been excited. A house was on fire and one of the people inside was critically injured.

'Does this belong to you?' a voice asked.

Beth hadn't even noticed a fireman approach her.

'Does what belong to me?'

A puzzled expression crossed Beth's face as she took what the fireman was holding in his outstretched hand.

A note rested in her palm. It was clearly charred from the fire and smelled heavily of smoke. Although the words were now smudged, Beth could read it clearly.

'It was too much.
I couldn't take it anymore.'

It seemed that Emma hadn't been the only one trapped in that house.

Throwing a cautious glance over to the house, Beth swallowed nervously.

This definitely wasn't over yet.

The Castle

Emma was surprised to see that nobody was in the great hall.

Where was everyone?

A screen had been placed in the corner of the room, next to the chest she knew contained spare dresses, uniform and items of clothing. This had been a tradition for years.

Opening the chest and rummaging through the box, it was then that she found it. Everything was going to plan.

Undressing and slipping into a scullery maid's outfit, she put the belladonna jar into one of the large pockets. Her own gown was carefully placed at the bottom of the chest, and Emma walked from the great hall.

She was ready.

Finally reaching the kitchens, she stepped into the bustling and busy kitchens area only to be shouted at, 'Where the hell have you been!' A woman with beady eyes and a permanent scowl glared at her.

'S-sorry,' Emma replied as meekly as she could manage.

A silver tray was shoved into her hands.

'Take that to the king,' the woman ordered.

Perfect.

Emma glanced at the tray in front of her and surveyed it quickly, on the tray was a plate of food and a flagon of wine.

Smirking, Emma produced the jar out of her pocket and tipped the poison into the flagon.

It would kill him in minutes.

Tiptoeing into the hall, she strode over to

194

the king and placed the tray in front of him.

'Wine, girl,' he demanded, not looking up.

'Yes, sire,' she muttered quietly, pouring the wine from the flagon into his goblet, watching carefully.

Emma stepped back into the shadows, eyes gleaming as he took a gulp and swallowed. It only took a few minutes for his head to roll forward and for his skin to turn chalky white.

'Night sire,' she whispered in his ear and placed a chaste kiss on his cheek.

Hearing commotion from outside of the great hall and the scream of the subjects, she paused and made her way away from the man. She didn't pause to see the king choke, his face transforming into an ugly royal purple as he did so.

Emma also didn't see the smoke rising in the village outside the castle.

Printed in Great Britain
by Amazon